TREASURE
TRAIN

NATHAN CROWN

CONTENTS

CHAPTER ONE

A BUSY DAY AT THE AIRPORT

The noise of tires screeching from the plane landing on the runway echoed inside the fancy lobby of the airport. The sunlight flooded the spacious, quiet area that was a homage to the arts. The minimalist design, modern furniture, and buttery-soft leather couches placed and positioned precisely over the creamy marbles, comprising gold and red hues, supplemented its extravagant look.

"This is the boarding call for passengers of flight 372A. Please proceed to gate 3."

Listening to the announcement, the crowd of passengers started assembling in front of gate three, falling in a line. A six years old boy, naïve and innocent, while walking to the terminal, stepped onto the freshly mopped floor, leaving his dirty little footprints all over it. His father pulled him back then and there as the boy giggled, unfamiliar with the mess he had made. He then turned towards the janitor mopping the floor a little further from their spot and called out,

"Listen! There, you? One mopping the floor!"

The janitor turned around and said, "Yes!"

"I guess you have to do it again, janitor."

Janitor sighed and dragged the mop to the footprints to clean them as he said, "My name is Stephen," in a low voice.

Stephen J. Foster has been working as a janitor for four years now. The guy is lean with average height, pale skin, and wide eyes. He must be in his early thirties. He is professional and never fails to report to work on time, wearing his shabby navy blue uniform. Working as a maintenance guy was not his dream job. Of course, no one wishes to work at the small airport of Fairfield, fulfilling the least significant position. The self-absorption of the people at the airport never annoyed him. The location of the airport is strategically important to serve the US Route 33 Business corridor, which isolates it from the central business district of the County. His concern was the nature of the work – loneliness, nonentity, and detachment. Not every job can be your dream job, but the little that it offers made the biggest difference in his life. The job paid enough for his bills and food, for which he was thankful, but the monotony was extracting all the excitement out of his life day by day – same place, people, job, and even payment with rotational hours and split weekends. He wanted a change that could inject the excitement back into reality. He couldn't accept 'janitor' as his only identity. He wanted to spend his life being more than that.

As he moved his wet mop over the floor, rubbing it against the footprints to remove them, the voices of an argument bought him back to his surroundings.

"Ma'am, open that suitcase!" The customs officer ordered in a stringent tone.

Stephen turned around to find the source of the voice.

"Why should I? It had already gone through the detector." The woman standing next to the metal detector gate cried. The lady appeared to be a foreigner due to her olive skin color and round hazel eyes. She was in her late twenties, carrying two large carry-on bags across the lobby.

"Ma'am! If there is nothing, then you shouldn't have an issue in letting us open it."

"The suitcase has my personal stuff, and you are opening it in front of the crowd. That's embarrassing," after finishing her sentence; the lady pulled the suitcase back.

"We apologize for the inconvenience, but this is part of the protocol." The customs officer answered her humbly. "If you wouldn't allow us to check it, then we can't allow you to take it with you. You may leave the queue for further verification process while we assist the rest."

The female customs officers stopped the lady and directed her to come out of the line. Then, two of the officers escorted her into the customs office for further investigation.

Stephen had witnessed all of this happening before as he has been working here for a long. He knew what was coming ahead after he watched her walking her away with darting eyes, arched eyebrows lowered, and knitted together. Mopping the floor step by step, he moved out of the lobby and ran into the storeroom next to the escalator. He locked it in a rush, opened the cupboard next to the door, and pulled out a stool. The room was dark, with a dim light illuminating in the center of the room. It only had some old used equipment and cleaning essentials. He placed the stool in the center of the room next to the ventilating duct. He then hopped onto the stool to remove the screws out of the steel sheet of the duct with the help of a screwdriver, with his palms sweating.

TREASURE TRAIN

As soon as he removed the sheet, he could make out some distinct voices. He leaned forward to hear them clearly.

"Ms. Stacy! You already know what's inside your luggage. Don't you?" This strict voice belonged to the same customs officer who was questioning the lady standing close to the metal detector.

"Officer! It's my personal stuff... kindly don't drag me into the mess." The lady appears to be rigid about her take.

"It's better to accept the offense rather than denying it and then getting caught red-handed." The officer tried to warn her, but it appeared as if she wasn't ready to cooperate.

"Officer, carrying luggage that has surpassed your detection machine isn't a crime. I should file a complaint against you for wasting my time. Because of you, I'll miss my flight! Now please let me go. If there was something in the luggage, the machines would have detected it in the first --"

The officer interrupted her, "ENOUGH!"

After a brief pause, he ordered the lady officer standing next to Ms. Stacy, "Officer Lisbon, kindly take the luggage from her and open it.... without wasting a minute!"

His tone made it evident that he knew what was inside the bag, and her denial infuriated him.

For a minute or two, the janitor couldn't hear anything. Then, he heard the office shouting, "How did two hundred thousand dollars end up inside the suitcase? What will you say now?"

"Sir... I don't know... It's not mine...I... I don't..." The lady tried to defend her position, but she was already held against the ropes.

"I don't need a word from you!" The officer barged in. "Confiscate all of her belongings and take her to the custom crime department for further investigation."

Stephen then heard some footsteps that ended with a loud bang from the closing of the door.

Stephen could hear the lady screaming to leave her and the lady officers dragging her out of the door. He immediately stepped down from the stool and rushed outside the storeroom. He then marched to the customs office with the cleaning equipment.

As he reached the room inside where Ms. Stacy was kept, he saw an officer coming out with the luggage. He stopped, looked into his eyes, and said, "Good morning, officer! I am here to clean the room."

"Yeah, right, Stephen. Make sure every spot shines when you leave. Good day." The officer walked away without giving attention to what Stephen was up to.

Stephen went inside the room and placed the cleaning equipment on the floor except for the gloves. He hid them in his pocket and went out of the room to follow the officer.

The officer walked swiftly to the other side of the lobby, where he went inside a password-protected room to hoard the luggage till the authorities could take it into their possession. For all this time, Stephen was following him. The plate hanging on the wooden door mentioned, "Private and confidential." Looking at it, Stephen was sure where was the money kept but for how long? To get his answer, he waited for the officer to leave.

As soon as the officer left, he went to the door and attempted to open it. The guard watching him rushed towards him and yelled, "Stop, Stephen!"

Stephen, who did it on purpose, moved back and asked, "What happened, sir?"

"You can't go inside! There is something confidential in there for the authorities."

"But last time when I went inside, I forgot something essential... now I need it." Stephen requested.

"Oh! I am sorry, but I can't help you at the moment." The officer smirked as if a janitor couldn't own something too valuable, but since he couldn't resist the tension on Stephen's face, he went on to say, "Can you come back on Thursday? Maybe I can help then."

"How?" Stephen asked inquisitively.

"The item inside will be moving out on Thursday, so you will be allowed to go inside for cleaning then." The security guard tried his best to assist him.

The answer bought a sparkle in Stephen's eyes as he said, "Sure... not a problem."

Stephen now exactly knows what, when, and where the key to the change lies that he has been looking for long to bring excitement back in his life. Now, he had three days to make all his dreams come true.

CHAPTER TWO
THE LAMB BECOMES A WOLF

By the moment the clock ticked twelve in the afternoon, Stephen was already tired of mopping the floors that would lose their shine the moment it was cleaned due to the increasing load of passengers and their visitors dropping by to bid farewell to their loved ones. However, this time Stephen was not concerned about the number of times he had pushed the cleaning trolley across the overcrowded lobby. It was his first day in life when his cleaning drill was not aimless. After taking seven rounds of the lobby, he walked to the shift supervisor, who was seated in the control room. Stephen knocked on the door, and one of the assistants opened it.

"Yes," the person answered.

"I want to meet Mr. Bakersfled," Stephen stated.

"Ah! He is busy right now...."

Stephen interrupted him and went on, "I know he doesn't meet anyone during the shift timings, but it's important... I have..."

While Stephen was making every attempt to convince the assistant to get to the supervisor, the door behind the assistant pulled back, and a tall bald man, more than fifty years old, carrying his potbelly, walked outside. As he saw Stephen, he started yelling, "Oh my goodness! What are you doing here during your shift hours? And then you will come to me claiming that you are the most dedicated person to work here... How do you show your dedication? By roaming around here and there at the airport, not doing your work, and disturbing the people who are actually trying to do something productive?"

Stephen's face turned red listening to Mr. Bakersfled, but this was not the moment to act on his emotions. He took a deep breath to calm his nerves and went on to say, "I am sorry, but I had to disturb you for this urgent issue."

As Stephen went on to talk to Mr. Bakersfled, he kept moving close to the door of the monitor room. While his lips were busy convincing his supervisor that he couldn't continue to work on today's shift, his eyes were peeking into the room through the narrow glass opening. Finally, he was successful in persuading Mr. Bakersfled.

"Stephen... this is the last time I am allowing you to get off before your shift ends, but I have to ensure that you don't turn it into a practice...."

As soon as Stephen opened his mouth to utter a word, Mr. Bakersfled cut him off, saying, "No excuses. You have to come back at night here. You will be posted with the night supervisor for the week, and don't confuse it with your duty hours. This is after you get done with your shift. You have to help him with everything, and by this, I mean everything!"

"I am...," Stephen tried to speak but again was stopped by his arrogant supervisor once again.

"I guess I was clear enough! NO EXCUSES!" He emphasized, "You must be thinking how you can be present on two-shift well you have to do only three hours in the night. You can praise me later for my mercy."

Stephen exhaled forcefully and said, "Sure."

Mr. Bakersfled rolled his eyes and went inside, mumbling, "Done and dusted. Now I don't have to attend night shift to help that good for nothing! My assistant will be there. Stephen, bring me some coffee before you leave."

Mr. Bakersfled laughed hysterically.

Stephen turned around and strolled to the kitchen to pour some coffee for his supervisor. As he dragged his feet to the coffee maker, his lips touched each other to widen into a deceiving smile. It appeared as if it was all he wanted to ask for from Mr. Bakersfled.

***

It was 11 am at night when Stephen again stepped back into the cold and hostile lobby of the Fairfield airport with a grin. He walked to the control room where Mr. Danny, the night supervisor, was waiting. Mr. Danny was a forty years old man, short and black, but he was quite considerate and tender than Mr. Bakersfled when it came to his subordinates. However, this was not the only reason behind Stephen's smile.

Stephen knocked on the door of the control room once again to report to Danny. Listening to the knock, Danny walked out of the room.

"Are you the one whom the morning shift supervisor sent in for my help?"

Stephen nodded.

"I thought he was going to come here on his own but never

mind. What kind of experience do you have?"

Stephen gulped as he went on, "I have been assisting Mr. Bakersfled for quite a few years in the control room task."

Danny smiled and went on, "Oh, that would be amazing! I am new here, and I would need a lot of help with the documentation, payrolls, and spreadsheets. Let's get inside."

Stephen knew that Mr. Bakersfled would never care to assist someone sincerely, so he didn't have to worry about Danny finding out his identity. The gun was on Mr. Bakersfled's shoulder since no ordinary employee had had access to the room before.

As he entered the control room, he saw 25 screens set up in a row right in the front displaying the visuals of every nook and corner of the lobby. One of them was right in front of the wooden door mentioning, "Private and confidential." On its left was a desk holding two computers and a label – an administrative desk. The room was spacious yet filled with monitors and other control room equipment leaving a narrow space to be seated. While he was observing everything inside the room, Mr. Danny called him, "Stephen! Come here to me."

Mr. Danny then made him sit on the administrative desk and asked him to prepare a list for employees enrolled in the night shift along with their designations and contact. It was the moment Stephen had been waiting since he cracked the secret of the possession locked inside the administrative room. Within an hour, the sound of the printer printing out the list bought a satisfying smile on Stephen's face. It was the list of the employees working at the airport. It is not difficult to presume that the pages did not only have the information of people working in the night shift.

***

The long arm on the clock strikes one. Danny, watching Stephen working tirelessly, asked him to take a break. As there was still an hour left in his shift to end, Stephen went out of the control room, hiding the copy of the list in his pocket. He walked to the storeroom and went inside on tiptoes. He doesn't have to worry about Danny following him to the storeroom since he disconnected the monitor for the camera towards this escalator. He then switched on the lights and opened the cupboard. Inside it was a large sheet, blue in color, rolled and folded. He pulled it out and unrolled it on the old wooden table.

TREASURE TRAIN

The header stated, "Ventilation structure of the lobby." Under it was a giant map indicating the spread of ducts across the lobby. Since the ventilation channel would spread all across the airport, this sheet was a blueprint for accessing the airport from each angle. Stephen smirked, moving his fingers down the ventilation channel established above the administrative room. He then secured everything carefully and placed it back inside the cupboard. It was time to return since some confidence was still left to be discovered. He picked up some coffee while going back into the control room. As he entered, he found the room empty. He then checked on the monitors and saw Mr. Danny walking in the lobby, moving to the bathroom. Stephen thought of it as a golden chance to seek the truth.

He immediately turned to the monitors and plugged in the cable to the administrative room. The screen started blinking with the message "ENTER THE PASSCODE."

"Damn! What could it be?"

He turned his head to see if Danny was out of the bathroom, but he luckily wasn't. He made two random attempts for the passwords, which obviously failed. Now it was the last attempt, after which the screen would be locked for thirty more minutes before he could make an attempt to enter the password again. Stephen was now getting anxious with every passing second. He looked all around the room but couldn't figure out anything that could help him. After wasting five more precious minutes, he recalled the glimpse of the keys of the administrative room that the customs officer had. The key had four digits embossed on it.

"This is a pure stroke of luck!" He thought as he typed those four digits on the screen. "Go, Stephen. This is it!"

The screen flashed "ACCESS GRANTED," and Stephen could now view the administrative room from inside. He again took a peek at the monitor showing lobby, but there were no signs of Danny. He made most of his time by observing the barriers that could stop him from getting to the confiscated cash.

"Bingo..." He jumped up in the air as he saw it was just a lock and password that was keeping him away from his dreams.

While rejoicing, he heard some footsteps coming to his room.

"No, not now...." He thought. As he turned off the monitor, he heard the door open behind him.

He turned around and saw it was another employee from the

maintenance.

"Inhale and exhale...." Stephen thought to himself. "Hello, Brother!"

The maintenance person walked inside with a blank face and said, "Oh, Stephen! I heard you will be helping the new manager today."

"Yeah! I have been trying to..." Stephen laughed nervously.

Stephen took a deep breath to relax over the fact that the monitor was turned off at the right moment. By the corner of his eye, Stephen saw Danny moving to the cafeteria over the other monitor. Of course, Danny was not going to be around for a while now.

"Well... where is Danny then?" The maintenance person inquired.

"He has been out for a cup of cappuccino...."

"Yeah! It's not easy to stay up all night shift without one..."

"I second you!" Stephen was sure that the maintenance person had suspected nothing as of yet.

"Okay, Stephen. I guess I have to go to the cafeteria to meet Mr. Danny. Enjoy your shift."

Stephen smiled politely as the man left his room. As he left, Stephen quickly arranged everything in a similar manner as it was before Danny left. All this time, he has been thinking about the lock and the key to it. While arranging everything, he thought about all other locks that had been installed around the airport for security purposes. However, all of them had a card to swipe to gain access. The lock that he saw on the screen appeared to be a similar one, but he had to be sure about it before he could move forward with the plan.

While Stephen was cleaning the mess he created, Danny came back.

"Hey, Stephen! It's been long. Hasn't it?"

Stephen chuckled, "it happens when you are awake all night, I guess."

"You can say. Well, someone came to meet me in the café, so I was kind of working during my break too...."

"Must be the maintenance guy. He came here too."

TREASURE TRAIN

"Oh! He didn't mention it, but who cares. I mean, my break time is gone now. I only care about it." Danny laughed to scorn. "Well... let's get back to work...."

Danny and Stephen went back to their seats. Danny started ordering Stephen to get the tasks done, and Stephen managed to follow the instructions imperatively. While moving the files, his eyes went to the clock. It was five minutes left to three.

"Mr. Danny, I will be off in five minutes. Let's finish this task, and you can assign the rest of the work to me tomorrow?"

Danny nodded in agreement. Stephen went out of the office to leave the airport, but this time he took a different route and went by the door to the administration room. He kept roaming around in the lobby for a while to notice the name tags on everyone's uniform present on their duties. He wanted to be sure about the list that he had printed on his night shift today, and he managed to locate most of them on it. He then went home to sleep over the struggles of his life for the night.

***

Stephen woke up to the sound of his alarm clock. The morning came as a promise kept unwrapping the wonderful hues over the sky. Stephen would usually wake up after this time, so he never had enjoyed this beautiful sight before. Looking at the sky while sipping his cup of coffee, he wished for all those colors to fill his life. He finished his coffee and was off to work early today. He only had today to figure out how to get through the door before the confiscated money would be moved. He boarded the train on the well-illuminated solar station, heading outside the city. It was cold, and the freezing breeze made him button his jacket while waiting for the next train. He always boarded on the fourth carriage from the front. He would usually survey his fellow passengers, which were few at this time of the day, and everybody he watched was concentrating on their task at hand, which was undoubtedly to get to their workplace. However, today his mind was busy with the thoughts of the lock. He knew the guard had access to the key card, but he was only allowed to use it after getting it assigned by the superiors for hours. For getting it assigned, the person had to submit his identity card till he returned the access key card, so this approach could lead him to a ditch instead of the treasure. Suddenly the train got into the Transbay Tunnel, and the noise level increased considerably, but that only meant he was very close to his destination. Finally, a few seconds before the train entered the station, he would get up and queued up to disembark. After getting off the train, he got into a bus that took him to the airport.

As soon as he reported to the shift, he found a professional lock maker working on one of the doors. He walked to the door maker and asked for tea to strike a conversation. The door maker refused but was now frank with Stephen. Stephen went on sharing his daily routine with the lock maker, and the door maker poured in his thoughts about life. As the door maker finished his task, Stephen went on to say,

"Sir, I was wondering if you ever feared computers and technology replacing us... especially you."

"How come?" The lock maker was confused.

"Well... now technology has been laid down its roots into everything, and it has even managed to get through your lock."

"Yeah! So?"

Stephen continued to explain, "Well, now they have locks with access cards. Don't you think this is a threat?"

The lock maker laughed. "Sir! A lock is a lock in the end... it's just the key that is different – it can be something made out of metal or electronic card, but once you lose the key, you will need these traditional tools to make it functional again."

"Loose the key... Traditional tools to make it functional...." These words kept echoing in Stephen's mind since the lock maker left. Stephen had finally figured out how to get to the treasure.

As soon as his shift was off, he rushed to his home. As soon as he reached home, he locked the door and jumped on the sofa to log on to YouTube. The answer that the lock maker gave had the best solution. Why should someone search the key when you can remove the whole lock instead? Stephen spent the evening watching videos on picking locks.

In a few hours, the stars filled the sky like pale corn into freshly turned ground. By this time, Stephen had already learned how to dismantle the lock, but the only area that he had to work on now was time. He would only have 30 minutes to go inside and move out while the security shift would change. It was still taking him 10 minutes just to dismantle it. However, the feeling of being so close to the destination kept him going. He continued practicing without a break.

After two hours, the clock struck twelve. Stephen was still

standing in his uniform, next to the door practicing to disassemble it against the timer. His stomach was roaring out of hunger, but nothing could move his attention. He was pouring heavily in his sweat, trying to save time.

"I can do it... I can..." He kept saying until it was 12:05, and he dismantled it before the stopwatch alarm went off.

CHAPTER THREE

THE GETAWAY

The sound of the alarm clock shook up Stephen to get up with the sun. Stephen wasn't looking as bright as the morning. The dark circles around his eyes proved his tiredness, but he lifted himself up with the never-ending energy as he saw the date on the calendar.

"Hurry up, Stephen! Today is the big day." He thought to himself as he rushed to the bathroom to prepare himself for the big day. After changing into his uniform, he searched for the bag that he had packed last night. He would carry a bag for essentials on a casual day, but today, the bag had specific gears to make his mission successful. He picked it up and strolled impatiently out of the house toward his destination. He took the same route, station, and train to the airport but with a new objective in his mind. As his ride went by, he kept looking across the window, admiring the time he had to spend waiting. Most probably, this was the last time he had been on his way to that dull and tiresome job.

As he reached the airport, he went straight into the storeroom.

TREASURE TRAIN

As he opened the door, someone called him.

"Stephen! You are on time. I am glad."

The voice took Stephen by surprise.

"Oh! That's you, Josh. Hi!"

"Yes. I am. Who else could have been here this morning?"

Stephen took a deep breath and went on to say, "Yeah. It's just that today is not my day...."

"Oh, really?"

"Wasn't able to sleep all night...."

"What kept this young man up, huh?" Josh winked as he placed the mopping solutions on the trolley.

Stephen chuckled. "Ah! A growling stomach."

"Aww... get well soon," Josh responded and left, pushing the trolley out of the storeroom.

"Phew..." Stephen rolled his eyes and rushed to the cupboard. He opened his bag and took out some torch, a small screwdriver, grease, gloves, a pair of jeans, and a top along with some screws and placed it inside. He then checked it for the wig and a colored disposable face mask.

"Everything appears to be in place," he thought.

He then placed the bag along with other bags on the shelf. Then walked out of the storeroom to report to Mr. Bakersfled. As he entered the office of Mr. Bakersfled, his eyes went to the clock.

"Mr. Stephen..." Mr. Bakersfled yelled behind him. "Or should I call you, Sir Stephen?"

Stephen stood there quite watching the clock.

"Look at me! You are late.... Not a minute or five ... but half an hour. Your manager is at work, and you have been snoring lying inside your covers. Awesome!"

"Mr. Bake.."

"No excuses! I am done dealing with irresponsible people like you.."

Stephen rolled his eyes.

"I guess he had a fight with her wife again... who would like to live with a man like that?"

TREASURE TRAIN

Stephen thought while Mr. Bakersfled kept on babbling over and over.

"So, I have a perfect solution for you. You will be posted in the administration today. First finish cleaning, then move to administration. There will be a lot of movement today as they have to move some items out of the airport... so you know I want the area to be neat and clean, shining like glass at the end of the day." He smirked.

"Sir!"

"No! Don't interrupt..." Mr. Bakersfled said, stopping Stephen from saying a word and going on, "You have to help Mr. Danny at night. I don't think you should go home today because you wouldn't be free before evening today."

"Yes, Sir!" Stephen snorted loudly.

"Yeah! You can thank me later for not deducting your salary for this. "

Stephen sighed and nodded.

"What are you waiting for? Christmas? Off to work!"

Stephen turned around and started walking to the corridor.

However, he had a large smile covering his face as he left. The area where he was posted after completing his tasks was the administration block, where the confiscated money was kept. He knew Mr. Bakersfled always had to punish people for petty issues. The punishment was the same. Always. Increased workload. As the customs would be moving confiscated items today so which other area could be busier than the administration bay? Stephen took the punishment on purpose. With a grin and under-eye bags, he dragged his trolley to the corridor to mop the floor, humming

***

After mopping the corridors back and forth twenty times, Stephen went to the storeroom. He picked his bag and walked to the administration to accomplish the incomplete task – mop and money. As he went there, he was assigned an identification number to enter. He submitted his identity details at the security checkpoint and entered the administration section. As he stepped inside the parameters, he saw a number of boxes stocked inside covered with the labels. The label stated the name of the item, the date, the item when the item was confiscated, and the code for the person it belonged to. Stephen was astonished to see boxes stating drugs, pistol, bullets, meth, firearm buckle, and much more. He walked slowly across the room with his mop and trolley in order to view each label. His eyes went from one box to the other in search of the box for cash, but he couldn't find it. He was now agitated by the thought of missing out on such a large amount of money as he couldn't track it using any source at the moment, be it person or machine.

"Hey, you janitor!"

Listening to this, Stephen turned around. It was a person from security.

"Yes," Stephen replied in a low tone.

"Go over to Area two and clean it! Now!"

"Alright." Stephen dragged his trolley silently to area two. As he was dragging the trolley, his eye went to the room next to area two. The room opened in front of him, and security personnel went inside with a bag along with his subordinate, ordering him, "Lock the cash bay as we walk out after keeping this bag."

Stephen smirked as he knew where the cash was now.

The day went by, and Stephen kept wiping off the dirty floor inside the chamber. It was two in the afternoon now, and everyone left for lunch. Before leaving, the security crew cleared the floor, making sure that no one stayed behind in the chamber alone or left with the items inside. Stephen has figured out the timings of the movement of the cash till this time. He still had 8 hours before the cash could leave the chambers, leaving his dreams into mere smoke. It was just a matter of two odds; when and how? However, Stephen wasn't a man who would show up at the stage without a plan.

After lunch, the crew returned to the chambers to finish the pending work. The next shift would take over their duties after five. Stephen managed to obtain the list of the employees in the second shift. He shuffled through the names where his eyes were caught by a name *'Peter Bernard.'* Peter was one of the airport security personnel who resembled Stephen by looks and physique. Ten minutes before five, Stephen sneaked into the IT department and made a call to Peter using the internal line since he knew the calls from this room were not recorded for security purposes. He informed Peter not to report in the evening today as his shift has been changed tonight. After the call, Stephen went to the storeroom and took his bag out.

***

TREASURE TRAIN

The orange hues of the skies were deepening, and the sunset came in its boldest blaze. Soon the television started to blow up with breaking news.

"Aviation reported a fraud of two hundred thousand dollars only to find out it was all plastic."

"The immigrant from Korea fooled Aviation by handling over fake thousand dollars."

"The airport security ended up confiscating two thousand dollars that turned into fake money overnight."

The airport security was dumbfounded when the customs department declared the confiscated money to be fake at the time of disposing it from the airport. Panic took over the air of the airport as all the managers and officers were called immediately. The news reporters started to gather at the airport to record statements from the Aviation Chief. The airport was completely sealed, and the flights were delayed so that not a single person could enter or exit the premises. Every person present on the shift was being interrogated. However,

Stephen was nowhere to be seen. Moreover, no one bothered him as he was part of the morning crew, but where did Stephen go?

Back at Stephen's place, he is seen sitting in front of the television holding a bottle of beer in his left hand, watching the news. A wig and a pair of glasses could be seen dropped near the sofa.

"Damn! It wasn't too late to find out. No?" he thought to himself.

He turned the television off. Holding the bottle in his hand, he walked humming into his room. He turned around, and his eyes sparkled, looking at his bed. A stack of 100 dollars could be seen scattered all over the mattress.

"That's all mine!" He screamed.

While the small airport of Fairfield was shaken by the turn of the events, Stephen slept peacefully over his messy mattress.

The next morning, it was a new day for Stephen. He woke up and dressed again in that shabby uniform. He knew well that he didn't need this job now, but he had to visit the crime scene to it wind up. After reaching the airport, he started his day with the same old mop and trolley humming and sweeping off the floor. He could hear the crowd and the crew gossiping, but he avoided becoming a part of the messy conversation. He met his colleagues showing disappointment over the event that took place last night and carried off with his day.

A week went by, and he kept up with the same routine. It was a busy Friday evening when Stephen was pushing his trolley over the freshly mopped floor and lost his control. Stephen fell over his back, dashing into the trolley with a loud bang. When his colleagues saw him lying on the floor, they rushed to pick him up, but Stephen couldn't move his legs. He was soon shifted to hospital. The medical professional advised him complete bed rest for twenty days till his legs were fine. Till the time he was on medical leave from the airport, he spent most of the time thinking about what he could do with such an amount of money. Occasionally, he would switch to television to follow up on the progress of the case.

"Ms. Stacy seems to be in big trouble." He thought and cackled. "Who is going to tell them that Peter did it?"

While watching the news, his mind went back to the time when the robbery took place. He chuckled over the fact that how he went into the chamber through the ventilation channels dressed up as Peter and moved the money out.

"Thank God I left early that day; otherwise, my night would have been ruined stuck at the airport."

He mumbled while thinking about how he left the chambers as Peter Bernard as soon as the evening shift took over. Lying on his bed, his life seemed dull. Being a Janitor wasn't an exciting job, but at least he had something to keep him busy. Being in bed all day reminded him how alone he was. In these twenty days, it was just one of his colleagues who called him to ask about his health. For the rest of the day, it was just his television, beer, and him. He felt himself drowning deep into the waves of depression. He felt as if there was a force holding him down to the bed. He became lazier day by day. On the nineteenth day, he finally found a plan to work on.

The next day, when it was time to leave his bed, he woke up and went straight to the medical professional. He bribed him to prepare a letter for his prolonged illness, which doesn't permit him to perform a job that requires standing for a long period of time. By submitting this letter to the airport administration the other day, he was officially relieved from the job. Mr.

TREASURE TRAIN

Bakersfled was quite happy to get rid of Stephen, and the happiness was mutual. Now he was free to go where he wanted to.

In the end, the secret of happiness is freedom, and Stephen has discovered it at least. However, freedom isn't free at all. Pain and loneliness are part of the price of freedom. With Mr. Bakersfield no more in the picture to slurp the happiness out of his day, Stephen realized that there was not much left to do. He once came up with the idea of working at a different place and setting, but all he could find was an odd job paying less while levying on his self-esteem. Money and bills were the only motivating factor for such jobs, but who would need it with a handful of cash in hand? Movies and drinks were barely helping him to survive the solitude. Fairfield was a small town, so he had already been to most of the places. Hence, there was nothing new for him to do. The air of the town now felt foreign to him; hence it became a deciding moment for him.

Standing on his terrace, enjoying a cup of coffee watching the cars passing by in the bleak evening, he thought, "Where can my restless soul find peace?"

He closed his eyes and started receiving glimpses of the places that he visited during childhood. Suddenly, it bought a wide smile to his face. He could see himself playing with his dad and siblings running over the green pastures in the cold breeze while he was young. He could see himself walking over the logs with his small feet holding his father's hand for balance. He could hear the voices echoing in his mind.

"Here, son! Take the aim of the rabbit... don't make sudden movements...."

The young Stephen nodded.

"Shoot your shot... Now."

The lively boy released the sharp stone launching it from his sling, hitting the bird sitting on the tree right on its wing, making it fall down.

"Good job, my boy!"

The proud father patted his son's back as both of them rushed to the wounded bird.

"You have a delicious dinner waiting for you tonight."

Stephen looked at his father innocently, unaware of what was going to happen next.

TREASURE TRAIN

"This is how you remove the skin...." Stephen looked at how his father cleaned the raw meat with his eyes wide open. At first, he was afraid of the amount of blood oozing out of the poor bird, but then he gathered himself to watch it.

With a sharp knife, his father cleaned and chopped the whole bird into pieces for the meal. Both of them then lit up some logs to roast the meat over it after marinating it in spices. Stephen admired the fire roasting the edible pieces hanging over it.

The honk of the car bought Stephen back to reality. He sighed, shook his head, and took a sip from his cup.

"Ah! This place will never allow me to breathe and relax," he thought.

He then went inside, placed a cup on the table, and sat over the rocking chair. He took a deep breath and rested his head on the back of the chair, and started rocking it back and forth slowly. He then again closed his eyes and began diving deep into his memories to kill his loneliness. He remembered the first time when his father took him to the cinema. The movie *Stalingrad* was newly released in the theaters. It was just the two of them since no one in the family appreciated watching battles and violence. He was mesmerized by the beauty of history. He always wondered how the people before him lived maintained peace and security. The way soldiers marched and fought over the borders for justice and rights fascinated him.

Stephen was himself a quiet and calm person. He couldn't gather much courage to raise his voice against people, so watching such movies encouraged him. Since then, he spent most of the time watching movies about World War I and World War II. As he grew up, he would save money to rent DVDs for new movies featuring events related to war and the events that followed. He inherited the fondness of such content from his father. His mother would often ask him to quit wasting money on movies and spend it on a good cause. However, he wouldn't listen till it was late.

A tear rolled down his eyes when he remembered how his mother took her last breath in his arms. The bus in which her mother and siblings were traveling met a horrifying incident leaving all of the passengers injured with four deaths on the spot. These four included his two siblings as well. All soaked in blood, he took his mother to the hospital, but he couldn't save her. She needed an immediate operation to stop the internal bleeding, but Stephen and his father couldn't arrange money for her on time. His father was a receptionist who tried his best to make ends meet and fulfill his children's wishes, but this saved him nothing. All he could do was wait for the angel of death to take his mother with him to end her suffering.

After that, his father spent most of his time alone, locked inside the room or wandering outside while Stephen would sit alone all day in front of the television, trying to keep his mind distracted from reality. His father would only be home when it was time for dinner – to cook and watch for Stephen if he eats. Even then, he would barely talk. Stephen grew up blaming himself for not saving the money. While watching various shows on television, he would try to search for information related to old hidden treasures. He then remembered the time when a show mentioned a lost train full of gold and fine art is hidden in the wilderness of Poland outside of Wałbrzych. Since the time he heard about it, he strived with all he had to get to it, but the struggles of daily life pulled him away from reaching his dream once again.

The thought of the train opened his eyes. He had to leave the thoughts of finding the train behind as the airport had been consuming him for a long time. However, the days of his struggle were over now, and he could get back on track for his dreams. With all this time on his hands, he could look for this train even if he found nothing he had close to a quarter-million dollars to fall back on. The idea sparkled inside his mind. He then picked up his keys to rush down to his vehicle. He took a can of soft drink with him to clear off his mind as he would drive his old ford ranger to think about his future plan. As he moved along the busy roads, he kept thinking about where he could start from. Then, suddenly, his vehicle stopped at a junction where he saw an advertisement board with the Statue of Liberty printed over it.

"Bingo!" He pushed the accelerator hard as the signal turned green.

"Woohoo! New York! Here I come."

CHAPTER FOUR
EXECUTING THE ESCAPE PLAN

After enjoying a lingering pause from mopping the airport and Mr. Bakersfield's arrogant sneers, Stephen couldn't wait to look beyond the beaten path. It felt like a perfect day to put the world around him at pause so he could play his own game. The thoughts of breathing fresh air in the bountiful parks, waterside golf courses, and riding trails kept him restless. However, the apprehensions don't induce him to make reckless decisions.

Stephen had a mind of a crow and the calmness of the sea. His boring job has taught him one of the most important lessons of life, "Safety comes first." He was clever enough to know that sudden resign, and migration could bring him on the radar. As impatient he was to run away from the diminutive town of Fairfield, he utilized all the means at his disposal to exit it without getting himself in trouble. While working at the airport, he didn't make many friends, but he certainly had made some important connections.

While moving items out of the storeroom, he would often see

an Algerian guy in janitor's uniform meeting travelers behind it. Whenever Stephen would find him in the middle of his private discussion, he would call it off and change his course. Stephen found it suspicious but didn't follow it as he knew that throwing stones in the mud could get his clothes dirty as well.

Once Stephen was moving across the corridor when someone accidentally bumped into him.

"Phew," sighed Stephen trying his best to stand, maintaining his balance as his left foot slipped over the soapy water.

As he turned around to see who did he bumped into, he saw some documents fallen on the floor. He knelt down to pick the documents up when two blue passports caught his attention. One was lying open with the page displaying the identification of the passport holder on the front. It said "*Name: Peter Luis.*" Out of curiosity, he rushed to pick up the other one when his hand collided with another hand of color. Stephen moved his gaze up to see who it was. He was astonished to see the same face that he saw behind the storeroom. As soon as their gaze met, Stephen hurried to pick up the second passport. As he quickly turned the pages, his jaw dropped wide open. The Algerian guy snatched the documents from him and rushed his way to the escalator. Stephen could see him running away with the proof but didn't move a muscle. The Algerian guy turned around to see Stephen and was relieved to lose his sight. He took the elevator upstairs and took a deep breath as he stepped off. At that point, he managed to run away from Stephen, but he didn't know what to do about his encounters later on. This thought bugged him a little, but then he thought that Stephen had nothing to prove his claims. For now, his main objective should be to get rid of these documents in his hand.

He strolled slowly to the bathroom at the back of the airport, which was in use by the general public. As soon as he stepped inside the bathroom, he locked it from inside. He then exhaled deeply and turned around. A chill went down his spine as he saw Stephen coming out from one of the cubicles. He hastened to unlock the door, but Stephen managed to get a hold of him.

"Leave me. Stay out of what isn't related to you," yelled the Algerian guy.

"I can't let you go until I find out everything," said Stephen tying his hands at his back.

The Algerian guy tried his best to get rid of Stephen's grip, but he couldn't.

"Enough!" called out Stephen as he punched his face. The blood oozing out of the Algerian guy's mouth cooled him down a bit.

Now he stood quiet tied with a urinal while Stephen went through all the documents he was running away with.

"How is it possible that both passports have the same picture but different names?" Stephen inquired with a smirk.

"You already know how, why, when... then why the hell are you asking it?" The Algerian guy replied, rolling his eyes.

Stephen punched him once again and said, "Shut up and answer me!"

"Okay.... I am associated with a hidden group that makes counterfeit passports and documents. I have been working with the alias Benni Noris. I have been collecting passports and documents from thefts. I go to hotels and find their suitcases and steal them when they're not paying attention. I keep the money if there are any, and if there are passports, I will sell them, and if there are Visa credit cards, I will use them up, and if there were any traveler's checks, I would use them or sell them."

"Bloody hell! For how long you have been doing it?"

TREASURE TRAIN

"1998..."

Stephen was looking at him with his eyes wide open. He moved close and searched his pockets. He found an identity car which stated his name as Paul.

"You aren't Paul. Are you?" Stephen questioned sarcastically.

"You can call me, Ressam."

"Interesting. I wonder why you never get caught," said Stephan keeping his hand under his chin.

"We are experts in falsifying documents, credit cards, and visas. This practice allows us to get legitimate passports using an alias, which will be basically foolproof at the border crossing. It is a huge international business, with brokers in China, India, Africa, and Central and South America. I am just a pawn in this huge chess game."

"The technology of counterfeiting is constantly improving, I see."

Stephen walked to him and took out a knife.

"What the hell are you doing?" Ressam shouted.

"Well... I was going to release you."

Ressam looked at him, perplexed.

"But before that, you need to agree to a deal..."

"What deal?"

Stephen continued, "You have to pay me a small amount of your commission every month, or I have the pictures of these documents that I can give it out in media...."

Ressam laughed. "You gotta be kidding me... people here don't care... you would get yourself in trouble."

"So what should I do? If I would just let you go, will you spare me?"

"Hmm... you can bargain your life for that documents instead of money."

"Isn't it better that I report you then?"

"No use. Every organization has mites, and so does yours. Those mites will save me... not you."

Stephen stood quiet for a while and then said, "This doesn't mean that I am gonna let you go without ransom."

"Then, let's do one thing... you get onetime payment and favor you can ask for any time in life. In return, you promise me my secret and privacy."

Stephen thought for a moment and then said, "Deal!"

While sitting in front of the television, he searched his cellphone for Ressam's number. He then found a number saved with the name of *Paul. R.* He dialed the number, and Ressam picked up. Ressam paid him the ransom as soon as he was released. However, Stephen hasn't asked for his favor yet, and now was the time.

"I want a name of my choice...." Stephen ordered.

Ressam chuckled, "Alright, mate...."

"How much would it take?"

"Two weeks and seven grand."

"What the hell!" Stephen wasn't ready to pay that amount.

"Ah! I am not keeping my cut... the price is for the process."

Stephen thought about it for a while, then agreed, "Do *Joshua Kincaid.*"

"Haven't thought of a birthplace?" Ressam taunted.

"Hmm... Austin, Texas? Maybe?"

Ressam laughed, "Something's never changing."

Two weeks later, Stephen received a parcel stating private and confidential. He opened it confused and surprised but was happy after unwrapping it.

"Finally! It's here," He exclaimed, holding his passport in his hand. Laying on the bed later that night, he wondered how fascinating it would be to spend these sleepless nights in the city that never sleeps.

***

It's a busy day at the airport when a row of passengers is seen walking in a line to board the plane.

"Everyone settle down on their respective seats as per their ticket numbers...."

Following the announcement, the flight attendants seated each passenger down. Among them was Joshua Kincaid looking out of the window.

TREASURE TRAIN

"Fasten your seat belts. The flight for Europe is about to take off." The announcement echoed inside the plane and bought a wide smile on Joshua's face.

"I deserve a vacation before I get to my destination," he thought to himself as the plane took off.

CHAPTER FIVE

ON HOLIDAY

Flight JFK 125 has arrived at Terminal 5. Passengers remain seated until further announcement."

The interval of two minutes seemed an eternity to Joshua. He unfastened the buckle of his seat belt as soon as he heard the announcement. He couldn't wait to get off the plane.

"Passengers may start unloading the flight. Please proceed to the gate on your right."

Joshua jumped up from his seat with excitement and headed to his right into the arrival terminal. Watching the planes and airfield through the glass walls of the departure lounge made him feel liberated instantly. He inhaled deeply to take a breath of fresh air in the enhancing atmosphere of London as he stepped out of the airport. He dragged his suitcases over the walkway as his eyes went across the widespread breath-taking views of the city. It was spring season, and the city already looked flowery and fun. The weather was perfect for strolling through the wondrous streets. He took a quick look at his watch.

It was the first time when had traveled outside of the city, and he didn't want to let go of the opportunity to explore the city. After catching a cab, he scrolled down the travel guidance platform to book a room in one of the luxurious hotels in the city over his smartphone. He made a perfect choice to select one near London's eye. At the sight of the millennium wheel revolving over the sparkling water of the South Bank of the River Thames, his heart began to dance with joy. The calmness of the river was thought-provoking. For all this time, Joshua's brain was hustling to find his true self and the purpose of his life. He decided to rest himself before continuing the journey.

Staying near one of the iconic London skylines, Joshua had plenty of options to look forward to. Therefore, he decided to start with his nearest option. Relaxing on the boat to enjoy the incredible views of the river was an underestimated experience. Joshua felt lucky to start his day with the boat tour. He hopped off at the other end of the Thames to visit the sea life in London Aquarium. It was a pleasure to eyes away from the dizzying heights and blazing lights of the busy city. The beautiful creatures housing the aquarium inspired the wannabe pirate inside him.

"Too much tranquility for the day," Joshua thought to himself as he began scrolling through his phone. "Let's get back to the adventure."

"London Dungeon is 0.6 kilometers to your north," said Siri.

Joshua wandered to the Dungeons, following the map. Live interactive shows always amused him. The thrilling underground rides were a cherry on the top. Among the laughs and screams, he did notice a group of tourists enjoying themselves. A wave of loneliness washed over him. Among them were middle-aged women of average height, brunette curly hair, and a wide smile. The sparkle in her eyes caught his attention for a moment. It was after a long time that he had noticed someone from the opposite gender after his teenage years. It was just once when someone took his heart away for a while but sadly, Joshua was unlucky in love. Joshua invested himself in a thought routine to move on from the heartbreak, and it was today when he decided to take some time off for himself. His eyes were different at the moment as he kept staring at the woman, softer than usual. Suddenly their eyes meet, and Joshua begins to feel embarrassed. His mind started comparing his average looks to the captivating eyes of the woman. While he was processing his thoughts, the woman smiled back at him.

"She has a pure heart," Joshua thought at himself and turned around to walk away. He was not up for emotional turmoil at this point in life. His drooping shoulders made it visible – he gave up too easily. He reached back to the hotel and decided to sleep over his misery before he could take off to the next destination.

After spending a busy and tiring schedule, Joshua had now become a slave to his loneliness. The thought of becoming a part of the crowd scared him. He felt comfortable as a spectator watching the show rather than becoming a part of it to take up the stage. He has learned his lessons the hard way, and he was not ready to walk the extra mile for strangers now.

To feel comfortable in his own skin, he decided to take a boat ride to France through the English Channel. He decided to float over the golden waves soaking under the bright sun to calm down. His old soul was a fan of the oldest way of getting to France - by boat. He booked a trip from Dover to Calais Ferry and hopped on to the boat around one noon. The ferry appeared glistening in the sunshine over the horizon.

Joshua sailed on the cruise taking great comfort in his own

company. The White Cliffs stretched along the shore game was a fascinating sight to enjoy. The whole range of amenities, bars, shops, and arcades made the trip a luxurious and pleasant experience. Enjoying a glass full of MSC Disarita while watching the glorious views of the Atlantic Ocean was a phenomenal experience to suit the tired old soul. It took him two hours to reach the other side of the shore.

"Bienvenue en France (welcome to France)," Joshua mumbled to himself as he caught sight of the port at the Opal coast.

The fine sand, dunes, cliffs, and breath of French air filled him with energy. He was ready to explore another area of the continent. While loading off the ferry, his eyes went to the iridescent grey light from the sky. He was awestricken by the sunlight falling over the blue seawater. The crew staff shook him to bring him back to the Earth from the wide skies. He was already smiling wide, leaving the port.

The vintage charm of the town attracted Joshua just like the aesthetic lovers around the world. The place had the touch of the Victorian era, which made enhanced the sophisticated design of the city. Even the cemetery was an outstanding sight to catch. For a person like Joshua, visiting it was just like walking through the past of the First World War and discovering its history, architecture, and construction. After the cemetery, it was time for the famous monastery. After a lovely afternoon visit to La Chartreuse de Neuville, his next stop was beautiful nature parks.

Growing up and living in the busiest cities of the United States, Joshua never had a chance to explore nature and wildlife. He was amused to explore this area alone, observe migratory birds and taste edible plants from the river's mouth. He then further went south, near to Berck-sur-mer, to Baie d'Authie, where he basked in the sun in the company of seals.

Now Joshua was hungry, so it was time to try its famed gastronomical traditions. No proper French meal is complete without a few verres du Vin. After having some, Joshua understood that it wasn't just the history and artistry that attracted people from around the globe. After fulfilling his desire for greener travel for two weeks, Joshua decided to loosen his roots in this place.

No doubt, it was an amazing escape to the countryside, but it never felt like home to him. He knew he had more places and sightseeing's to delve into. His next stop was Germany.

Entering Germany was not so easy during this time because of Covid-19 travel restrictions, so he arranged a car along with an agent that would help him to cross the border.

Joshua left the inner areas of the city right before midnight. While the agent was driving the car to the borders, he peeked outside the window, looking at the sky and thinking, "I am ready to go where life takes me...."

Joshua logged on to the google map to watch himself moving across the roads. His eyes went to the number of kilometers and time it would take to make it to his destination, and he was a bit disappointed.

"Well... never mind!" He sighed. He could afford to show patience for a ten hours journey by road when he knows that there is nothing waiting for him on the other end. He was a free bird, traveling to stretch his mind and perspective. He peaked outside of the window and saw five or six SUVs moving at a similar speed. Usually, the route is busy, but due to the pandemic and the fact that he was traveling at night, it was not crowded out there.

TREASURE TRAIN

He, for an unknown reason, enjoyed the quietness. His bourbon decanter perfectly complimented the peace and joy of the road trip. He took a sip and kept looking out at the trees and signboard that he was leaving behind while moving forward. He was really glad to leave a number of issues behind.

Joshua finds it relaxing looking out at the clear skies and shining stars in the middle of the night. He looked at the watch, and it was 4:30 am. He was finding it difficult to keep his eyes open, so he rolled up the windows of the Citroen Grand Picasso that he was riding and straightened his back in the backseat to catch some sleep. After a blink or two, Joshua falls asleep. The driver could now hear him snoring, but he was accustomed to giving rides to people at night.

**

Joshua woke up from the rays of sunlight shining on his eyes. He rubbed his eyes as he tried to look with his blurring vision. He could feel his head heavy, "I shouldn't have drank that much last night..." he thought to himself. He stepped out of the car, smudging the sleep dust out of his red-rimmed eyes, and his jaw dropped down open to what his eyes saw. He was standing right in front of the Vaux-le-Vicomte. The French Chateau was a fantastic stop to freshen oneself up from a tiring road trip. The Chateau was famous for to inhabiting spirit that would welcome each visitor as a guest during the late 1960s. The Chateau is well known and has an inhabiting spirit that welcomes each visitor as a guest. Joshua, filled with the anticipation of seeing the place for himself, he hurried towards the front entrance.

Joshua, quite excited to meet one, rushed towards the entrance front. As he entered the Chateau, he found it decorated and furnished with the rare decors that have remained intact since the seventeenth century. His eyes were resting upon the majestic views fashioned from Medieval, Gothic, Renaissance, and Classical facades. The perfectly symmetrical elevations, the entrance vestibule to the north and the oval salon to the south, the three sets of three arches offering a view of the central axis of the garden, and the delicate glass door and mirrors made it a perfect construction to please the eyes. The Chateau was organized into four levels, and Joshua was pleased to visit all of them one by one. Joshua was eager to visit all of them one by one. After he went across all the levels. After he went across all those levels, he strolled up to the central dome. The dome offered him a breathtaking panoramic over of the estate from twenty-five meters above the ground.

It was past twelve in the day now, and the sun was directly over the head. Joshua grabbed some sandwiches and drinks at Relais De Lecureuil. After satisfying his taste buds with some flavorful drinks, he was back in the car to continue the rest of his journey. He watched the clock tick by, but this time they were moving slower since it was afternoon, the Sun was overhead and the amount of traffic had increased on the road. All this means, he had ample time to think about what he could do as soon as he got to the other end. At first, he thought about getting some rest on a cozy bed since his back was hurting after sleeping in his car. Secondly, he was thinking about enjoying an amazing dinner as he was really hungry after this never-ending long journey. Then, he decided to book a hotel without wasting a single minute before he could reach his destination. As he started surfing the net, he saw the websites displaying their content in German.

"Oh! How can I not think about it?" He mumbled.

He then scrolled down to find a way out of it. Luckily, some websites did offer an option to convert the text to English. This is how he was able to make a reservation for his room. After processing the order, he sighed and thought about what he would do after reaching Germany since he didn't know how to speak even a bit. He thought about it for a while, and then his frowned lips started turning into wide smiles. He hunched into the front and asked the driver how soon they can reach Germany. The driver replied, "Six hours."

"Enough to make this work!" He thought.

He then unlocked his cellphone and started to translate some common sentences into German. He then pressed the speaker icon to hear how these sentences are spoken. He spent almost all of the journey left learning the basic vocabulary of German, and by the time his car was about to end in Germany, he knew most of the everyday spoken words; hello, how are you, thank you, where is this, what is this, etc. The only struggle left now was to understand the reply of the German that he left on his luck to make some sense out of it.

Joshua fell in love at first sight with the capital of Germany as soon as he arrived. Berlin appeared just as the city of his dreams. It had everything that he was looking for in a city adventure for someone on the loose. Upon stepping out of the

TREASURE TRAIN

SUV on the other side of the border, he asked the driver for favor with a persuasive smile. Of course, the driver couldn't say no to book a cab on the phone for Joshua, especially when he was making some extra bucks out of it. Who said that money couldn't solve problems?

Now Joshua was off to the hotel to rest. Riding alone was never trouble for him. An ultimate classic rock from 'The Beach Boys' could turn a boring drive into a fun ride for him anytime. Within two hours, his cab was standing right outside a modern four-star hotel that was situated directly opposite Europe's largest landscaped animal park. Joshua's jaw dropped open looking at the aesthetic structure of the building – Shining glass walls, contemporary pillars, and support, minimalist circular ring chandelier at the entrance.

"Woah! Never thought an animal park could flatter me this far away from my country," He mumbled.

One of the hotel's guards understood English and helped Joshua understand and pay for the ride. Joshua thanked him and went inside while the guard kept staring at him weirdly as he walked inside the hotel. At the reception, one of the translators helped him and escorted him to his pre-booked room. The porter followed them to his room and left after getting a wholesome tip. As Joshua locked the door, he jumped on his bed and sniffed the blanket.

"AH! The smell of luxury," he thought. Exhausted from the road trip, his tiredness was heavy enough on his eyes to shut them down for a good nine hours. Joshua slept like a baby in the same clothes in which he made a trip across the border while his luggage still rested next to the door.

After crashing out, Joshua's eyes shut opened in response to the ringing of the intercom. He looked at the round wall clock hanging on the white wall. The larger hand was at nine.

"Oh my god! I guess the party must have started by now."

He jumped out of bed. He gave a second thought about answering the intercom but as soon as he reached for it, it stopped ringing.

"Never mind!" he mumbled and rushed to the bathroom to get ready to enjoy the night. Who would miss the opportunity of having a wild town in the party capital of Europe? He joined the buzzing night in one of the famous city clubs. Amazing drinks and the club with no closing time meant "fun for eternity."

TREASURE TRAIN

After some drinks, Joshua took the stage with DJ on epic beats for the night. While Joshua moved his body to the rhythm, a group standing across the floor on the bar stool watched him while whispering to each other. As Joshua got down from the stage and walked to the bathroom to release the building tension inside in pants, one of the men in the group, slim-fitting a button-down collar shirt in check, nodded to the other in plain. The group stood out from the rest of the crowd since their heads were shaved. The man in a plain shirt followed Joshua inside the bathroom and locked the door.

He waited outside the cube for Joshua to come out. As Joshua came out after taking a piss, the man held him with his right arm and pressed him against the wall.

"What's the problem, gentleman?" Joshua asked with his hiccups adding pauses in his sentences during the whole conversation.

"You," the man said while grinding his teeth.

Every question that the bald guy would ask, Joshua would just chuckle in response. Joshua couldn't make sense of the situation, partly because of alcohol but mostly because he himself didn't know what was going on. After manyin quite a few vain attempts, the guy punched the life out of Joshua's face twice. With the blood and a molar coming out of his mouth, Joshua was back to his life on Earth. He realized that he was in grave danger.

"What's your problem, Mr. Whoever?" Joshua inquired furiously. Again, this wasn't Joshua speaking. He knew how to handle a heated conversation, but this time, it was the alcohol taking over his communication skills. Such a question dragged him further into difficulties since the guy was much taller and more muscular than him. With each punch, the guy asked Joshua to think about what he had done wrong in the past three hours. All he could recall was getting ready, boozing, and dancing. As he received a hard punch in his stomach, his mind went to the call that he didn't receive. But how just not picking up one call can make a bald guy this crazy. Nothing made sense for him at the moment.

"You are doing the wrong guy," Joshua finally came to a conclusion.

The bald guy chuckled and yelled, "Yeah! Now you would know who was wrong."

As the guy pushed Joshua across the floor, Joshua landed next to the exit door. He gathered himself and stood up to open the door as fast as he could. Somehow he managed to make it to the lock and escaped the bald man catching his breaths in between with great difficulty. As he ran out, the group of the bald guys was already waiting for him.

A chill went down his spine, looking at the muscular group. He knew he was in grave danger. As he observed all of their faces one by one, he realized one of them was on the stage while he was displaying his dance moves.

"Oh! You jealous of my dance move?"

Again, the alcoholic answer bought a gift for Joshua as one of them held Joshua from his neck. Another in the group started kicking him while shouting, "How dare you throw drinks at me? Huh! You immigrants think that you can come here and spoil our parties. This is our club! Our night! You are not welcomed here."

This reminded Joshua of what he could possibly have done. While he was dancing, he waved his hand to the glasses that the bald guy was holding. As Joshua wasn't among the people who would let his ego eat him alive, he said sorry immediately at that particular moment. But the way the bald guy reacted didn't appear as if he accepted his apology. The bald guy started swearing at him. This was the moment when the drinks started acting up on Joshua, and he decided to answer his response by following a simple rule – an eye for an eye. He spilled more of his drink on the bald man and said, "This time, I am not sorry." Then, Joshua went to the floor. The bald guy wanted to follow him, but his group stopped him. At that moment, Joshua thought the group had stopped him and he had solved his problem, but only to realize now that they were back to give him a rock-hard answer. He gulped, looking at his man's face, who was coming closer to give him another punch.

CHAPTER SIX
REISEN DURCH POLEN (TRAVELING THROUGH POLAND)

Joshua was running away frantically for his life; there was no way he could counter the bulky group of germans all on his own. He knew he had bitten more than he could chew.

Without a moment's hesitation, Joshua decided that the best course of action would be to hide or divert their attention. He ducked behind a garbage bin, hoping they would pass by him. Joshua was almost successful with his plan; however, the bald guy that had punched him earlier looked through the corner of his eye and stopped.

"I don't think he had run away; no one can run away that fast."

"What are you suggesting? Do you think he's here somewhere?"

The group spread out in hopes of finding Joshua. Beads of sweat transpired on Joshua's forehead as he realized they would locate him at any moment. He didn't have the energy to fight more, especially a bunch of drunk hooligans. Quietly, he crouched down lower to hide his shadow. His strategy worked, and luckily they passed by him.

"He must have gone that way, behind the bushes. Spread out, guys; I want to make him sorry for ever messing with us." They ran past the garbage bin and were soon out of sight.

Joshua let out a sigh of relief and got out of his corner. Quietly but hurriedly, he made his way back to the hotel. Finally, back at the hotel, he found some solace. Recounting the night's events, Joshua couldn't believe how the night had transpired.

What was meant to be a fun trip and a night to get laid back left him injured and bleeding. However, this was one of life's adventures, and he couldn't start complaining. Compared to all that he had been through, this was blissful. His mind was busy with grateful thoughts as he slid into a deep slumber.

Joshua slept peacefully till daybreak, and the knock of the room attendant making their morning calls woke him up. Disgruntled from last night's episode, he was still experiencing a hangover. His head was spinning, and there was dried blood on his face from the blows of the bald guy. Looking at his face in the mirror, he could hardly recognize himself. His left eye was swollen shut, with bits of dried blood sticking around.

TREASURE TRAIN

Meanwhile, his head was spinning very fast, as if a batsman had hurled a ball at full speed. Only the ball was his head.

"Ughhhh," He let out a disgruntled moan and attempted to get out of bed. Even the most menial tasks were taking effort. Joshua pulled himself together and got out of bed; he had to be resolute. No one else was coming to save him; this much was clear. Making his way toward the bathroom, he washed his face.

"Ouch" It stung, but he kept going on. He had to get his wound before it became infected, which had already been long enough. Joshua bandaged himself and treated his wounds, taking supplies from the first aid kit. He called the hotel's restaurant for some breakfast; he needed to build his strength.

After a hefty breakfast comprising a cheese omelet, beans, bacon, and coffee, Joshua felt more like himself. He began to think carefully about his next plan of action, as he couldn't afford any more setbacks. His goal was to travel through Poland and into Wałbrzych. It was pertinent that he reached his decision; otherwise, a lot could go wrong.

He took out a piece of paper and began jotting down his next course of action in bullet points. Checking his wallet, he saw that he had little to no cash. He thought this wouldn't be enough for his trip to Wałbrzych.

Contemplating his options, he knew there weren't a lot of options left. His journey had to be made on foot. This wasn't going to be an easy task; he would need ample food and water to make the journey. He let out a long sigh; he wished he had the money for his trip. But there was nothing he could do; he could have stayed a few days longer in Germany and saved up while getting a job, but he didn't have the time.

He needed to move quickly. By nightfall, he packed his bags and checked out of the hotel. The hotel attendants helped him with his bags and inquired about his transport.

Joshua politely informed him that he would make the rest of the journey on foot. The attendant gave him a weird look, handed him his bags, and was on his way.

Joshua sighed; he was sadly used to this behavior. Whenever the world was presented with something out of the box or even remotely different than the norm, they refused to accept it. Determined, he set out with his bags on his shoulders and walked towards his destination.

Joshua took out his phone from his pocket and typed the

coordinates of his destination. Within minutes he had the directions of his new journey in front of him. Joshua began to walk along the empty road, taking in the scenic view. The bird chirped in the distance, and it was a beautiful sunny day.

Personally, Joshua loved walking around and exploring new attractions, but today he had a new mission in mind. Luckily, he had enough money to survive his journey; he had gotten some food, water, and other essentials from the hotel, which were included in his room. The trouble was that he needed to visit a money changer to convert his pounds into zloty, the native currency of Poland.

Joshua had walked over a mile now; however, there was still no sign of money exchange or a bank. His phone was also running low on battery; he had to find directions quickly. Otherwise, he would be left stranded on the roadside without any provisions. He continued walking in search of a subway station or a rest house, a place where he could ask for directions and charge his phone. Looking down at his phone, he saw that it was only left with 5% battery; it would die down any moment. Quickly, Joshua typed in the instructions to the nearest subway station. The nearest one was about 10 minutes away. Blessed to have a photographic memory, Joshua quickly noted down the direction in his mind. He was entirely on his own now, not that he had any actual company before. However, he preferred it that way.

Joshua was an intelligent being who had been living independently for quite a while now and had gotten used to this routine. He didn't like the idea of relying on another being, especially a human one.

Before he could forget the direction, Joshua darted quickly towards the subway station. It was deserted, thankfully. He half-expected the group of bald guys searching for him there. Seeing the place half-empty, except for some homeless people sleeping on benches, the place was isolated. He quickly went over to the maps and located the nearest bank.

The subway station was starting to get busy as more and more people wanted to catch the next train. He wrote down the directions to the nearest bank on a notepad while his phone was on charge on one of those portable charging ports. As soon as his phone was about 20%, he started walking again towards his destination. Joshua reached the bank in less than the estimated time through the instructions he had jotted down on his notepad.

TREASURE TRAIN

The bank was located in a secluded suburban neighborhood, a new white marble building that stood apart from the cement houses. People were going in and out, catering to the needs of their daily routine. Joshua made sure to keep a low profile; he didn't want to attract any unwanted attention. He couldn't afford any other fiasco, similar to the one in the bar. That was truly a scary night.

His thoughts racing fast, Joshua entered the bank. With a quick scan of the room, he could see there were little to no people in the lobby. This should be quick, he thought to himself. He made his way to the money changer and presented his pounds in exchange for zloty.

The lady sitting at the counter eyed him from top to button, judging his casual appearance.

"Do you have your Id on you, Mister?"

"Joshua, and yes." Swiftly he pulled out his wallet from his bag and gave it to her. She peeked through her thin glasses, first at the Id card, then at Joshua. She was making sure that both were the same person. For some unknown reason, Joshua felt nervous around this woman. She seemed to be looking inside his soul, hoping to catch one flaw, one offense he had done so that she could hand him over to the police. Finally, after finding nothing, he handed him his Id card back.

Her face was more relaxed now, and she asked him: "Would you like an envelope for that?"

"Yes, please," said Joshua, managing a small smile. He felt much more relaxed now that his scrutinization was over. Joshua was out of the bank and on his way in a few minutes.

He wouldn't let anything stand in the way of his destination. It was highly crucial that he reach the outskirts of Wałbrzych by nightfall; otherwise, it would take him much longer to reach the city. It was almost twilight, and he had only a few hours left.

Outside the bank, there were several benches for passersby to rest in. Joshua seated himself on one of the benches and took out some sandwiches. He had been travelling since morning, and his stomach was now growling. Hungrily, he started chewing on the sandwich and drank some bottled lemonade with it. Joshua was so hungry that he wanted to eat the second sandwich he had asked the hotel staff to pack had packed. However, no stores were nearby, and he knew he would get hungry again in the morning.

TREASURE TRAIN

Joshua's plan was to camp outside the outskirts of Wałbrzych. While getting his money at the bank, he had estimated that he had enough money to stay at a hotel. A warm hotel room would be so much better than living at the edge of the forest, at the mercy of wild animals. However, he had been gravely wrong. The hotels in this part of the town were much more expensive; it seemed he was camping outside.

He contemplated this for a little while; however, his thoughts were soon interrupted by a small orphan girl. She was standing next to him as if asking permission to sit beside him. Joshua looked at her warmly and nodded his head. Whatever he was, he was not an unkind person.

The little girl sat down beside him; Joshua was looking at her intently. She had a tattered pink dress on, which felt like it hadn't been taken off in ages. Her hair was tied up in a matted braid. But the thing that intrigued Joshua the most were her eyes. They were big and brown, and had an unnatural hope to them.

The only puzzling thought that came to Joshua's mind was this girl, an orphan, had so much in her eyes in a world that had treated her so unkindly. He contemplated his life, it hadn't been easy, but he was sure it was so much better than what this girl was used to. At that moment, Joshua felt grateful for what he had and how his life had turned out. On an impulse, he took out his second sandwich and handed it to the girl. Seeing the happiness in her eyes made him feel blessed. He wished he could capture that moment.

Leaving the girl on the bench, Joshua started walking again. It was almost nightfall now; he should have reached by now. Luckily, he wasn't that far from his destination and reached it after thirty minutes of walking.

The gates of Wałbrzych were now visible from a distance. Joshua camped at the outskirts. It was a woody area, peaceful and calm. He set up his tent and laid out his sleeping bag inside, preparing for bed. Joshua set the alarm for 5 in the morning, as he was excited to get inside the city. Also, it wasn't safe to lie out in the open like this for a long time.

With these thoughts in mind, Joshua dozed off to sleep. His mind and heart were excited ~~for~~ about the next day's adventure.

CHAPTER SEVEN
SETTING UP CAMP

Joshua woke up in the early hours of the morning, disgruntled and groggy. Although he had camped out several times, it wasn't comfortable this time. His sleep was riddled with nightmares rather than pleasant dreams, and he kept waking up due to the voices in the forest. Feeling scared that an animal may attack him, he was restless throughout.

He terribly missed the comfort of the hotel room and regretted his decision to camp out instead of getting a cosy room. He forced his mind to wake up, slapping his face to numb out the drowsiness. Joshua felt an intense need to go to the washroom and wash his face. Sadly there wasn't going to be a portable bathroom in the middle of nowhere, *think practically*, he thought to himself.

Joshua started walking in hopes of finding a solution to his dilemma. Soon enough, he came across a stream of fresh flowing water nearby some thick trees. *This will have to do for now.* He thought to himself and proceeded to do his business. Cleaning himself from the steam's fast-flowing water, Joshua felt refreshed. Now we need to do something about food, his stomach was starting to growl, and he felt hungry. Unfortunately, he had run out of food supplies the previous night, even though he had enough money to buy some snacks. Looking around, it was apparent that there wasn't a general store or a bakery anywhere in his line of sight. It wasn't as if he didn't have money; however, he had run out of the local currency and would have to go to the money exchange again. Unfortunately, they weren't around on this path that he had taken.

Sighing to himself, Joshua scanned the trees looking for some fruit or vegetables. He broke a reedy branch from a small tree, fashioning it into a makeshift fishing rod with sharp rocks from the forest floor. This done, he plunged the rod into the heart of the stream, exclaiming with joy when he came across two fish at the other end. *This will do for lunch;* he glanced at the sky; *it just as well is lunch at this point.*

Gathering some rocks and more wood, he started a fire to cook his fish. Joshua had successfully also collected some berries and vegetables he planned to eat and cook with the fish.

Soon enough, Joshua had ignited a blazing fire that burned

heartily with the help of the lighter. Over the years, due to his nomadic lifestyle, he had acquired a particular set of skills that allowed him to be adaptable. He could prepare five-star gourmet meals from this simple fire, fish and a handful of vegetables. This may seem extravagant, but he was an avid foodie even though his lifestyle didn't always allow him to enjoy the luxuries in life. Joshua, didn't want to compromise on meals, as it directly pertained to his health. He needed to keep his health up. Otherwise, his enemies would finish him off in mere seconds. He couldn't afford to take that risk. Hence he tried to keep his diet varied, incorporating a balance of proteins and carbs.

While cooking, he reflected on the previous night's nightmare. He still remembered it distinctly, as if it was happening to him in stop motion. He was stuck in hell, and it was World War II again. To make matters worse, he was the alleged criminal being chased by SS soldiers who were thirsty for his head. The soldiers had bayonets on their guns and kept firing rounds at him. Joshua was running for his dear life; even now, when he remembered the dream, it gave him goosebumps all over his arms.

In the dream, he remembered feeling hopelessly alone; no one was willing to help him. He kept running to lose sight of the soldiers, but they never stopped chasing him. All the civilians shied away from him, careful not to ignite the government's wrath upon themselves. He still remembered looking into pairs of cold eyes as he begged them to shelter him. However, no one was willing to offer him refuge, as it was a huge risk for their own family.

He finally found refuge in some big bushes, which provided a temporary shelter and saved him from his sad demise. As he hid in the bushes, Joshua could hear his heart beating faster as he prayed for the soldiers to pass him by. They would surely kill him right on the spot if he were discovered.

However, just as he was about to relax and breathe a sigh of relief, a soldier spotted him and stabbed his bayonet sharply in Joshua's chest. Joshua knew there and then that he was done for if he didn't act fast. He would shoot him right here or alert his comrades if there was a scuffle. Just as he was racking his brain to escape this dilemma, the soldier pressed the gun harder into his chest, just above his heart.

Joshua remembered gulping as he prayed to the gods above to spare him. Although he wasn't particularly religious, at that moment, he was prepared to believe in anyone who would offer him respite.

As if his prayers were answered, Joshua woke up at that very moment safe and sound. Although he was still shaking from his ear death nightmare, he was unharmed in his sleeping bag. He peeked outside just to make sure that he wasn't being followed or there was no imminent danger at his tail. Once making sure that he was truly all alone, he slumped into his sleeping bag in the middle of the forest. Dozing off to sleep once again.

Joshua came back to reality after replaying last night's incidents in his mind. He absentmindedly traced his hand on his chest, thinking to find a puncture wound there. However, there was nothing there; he breathed a sigh of relief. He finished his breakfast quickly and packed his makeshift house. But before disrupting it, he gave one last look to his ~~handywork~~ handiwork and felt proud. Even though he was out of practice, he had managed to make a pretty sturdy wooden structure for the night. For his tent, he had used light branches that were easy to lift and break but were also good enough to support his weight. He had comfortably placed his things inside while also making sure that he would have enough room to sleep without banging his head on the roof.

Even though he had repeatedly tossed and turned in his sleep, he had been lucky enough not to bang his head. Joshua smiled as he collected the sticks one by one, and disposed of them randomly. He was smart and calculative, as he didn't want anyone to follow in his footsteps in case anyone was tracing him.

He still had about six to seven miles still left till he reached Walbryzch. It was morning, and he wanted to reach there by mid-afternoon.

Joshua walked along the pathway comfortably; he wasn't in a mood to rush the journey. Although he wanted to get to Walbryzch quickly, he knew that hurrying on foot would only make the trip harder. There was so much he could achieve with his limited resources. So it was best that he enjoyed the walk in the middle of the forest and admired mother nature's handy work. He took his sweet time observing the woods, watching the different kinds of flora and fauna that breathed on the forest floor. Looking at it from the lens of daylight, he realized that he had nothing to worry about. The forest was harmless, and it was his own fears that troubled him all night.

As he walked, he came across a clearing and was too stunned to continue. It felt as if he had stumbled upon some kind of utopian illusion. The scene before his eyes was no less than a movie set. Before his eyes was a sapphire blue lake that sparkled in the sunlight. Surrounding this glorious water body were all kinds of plants and flowers. Even the air smelled sweeter. Joshua sat on the ground as if in a transfix, keeping all his things beside him. He was shocked at how peaceful it was, right here at this very moment, and he wanted to cherish it.

He had been on the run his whole life, never truly enjoying the small details of life – and he enjoyed that lifestyle. The thrill, that adrenaline that came rushing to his heart whenever he heard that he was yet again wanted. Whether it was the police or roadside thugs, Joshua was always up for a challenge.

However, he felt that something was changing inside of him. He wanted to settle down and live a quiet life. Probably with himself or maybe even a family. He was tired of being alone; truth be told, he didn't have the agility he possessed years ago.

Joshua looked at the time on his watch; it was almost mid-day, and soon it would be time for lunch. Instead of starting back on his way to Walbrzych, he decided to explore the woods a bit more. He would be a fool to give up on this scenic route and go back to the urban city.

Looking at the hills, Joshua thought it would be a good idea to hike. The weather was perfect, and he could do without the hustle and bustle of the city for one more day.

Work can wait; let's enjoy ourselves for once. It was surreal, the deafening void of humans, being completely alone. All by himself, Joshua felt at peace after a long time.

CHAPTER EIGHT
GETTING A LAY OF THE LAND

Joshua trudged along the steep hill, he didn't know where the path was leading him, but he wasn't worried about it. For the first time in a long time, no one was chasing after him.

He knew this wouldn't last long, so he cherished the moment. After all, he was a fugitive on the run, a criminal who could find no solace anywhere.

Every step he took felt a like he was freeing his soul from the shackles of crime. He climbed the hill for half an hour more until he reached the top. The view from the top was breathtaking. Joshua was too stunned to climb all the way down again immediately. He decided to just soak in the amazing beauty that surrounded him.

He placed his bag on a huge boulder and climbed on top of it. Atop the boulder, Joshua could see everything. The skyline of Walbryzh was visible. For a few minutes, he stared in the distance looking at his destination from afar. It was beautiful, yet it didn't bring him comfort. He felt nothing when he saw the city; it was just a place where he had to go and complete his plan—nothing more, nothing less.

Joshua was emotionless when he stared at the city; relatively, he was feeling more here at the boulder. Not exactly emotional, but more so at peace. For some stranger reason, this place felt like home.

Deeply buried in his thoughts, Joshua began to get drowsy. He took out his sleeping bag and pillow, placing them in a comfy spot, before falling fast asleep. He decided to take a quick nap before going to look for the lost train.

At first, he slept soundly, like a baby. However, soon things began to take a more tumultuous turn. He began to shift in his sleep. Usually, this wouldn't have been a big deal. However, he was on top of the boulder, which was perched precariously at the corner of the hill. One sudden move and Joshua would stumble to his death. This sudden, horrifying reality, however, was unnoticed by Joshua, who was too busy reliving his nightmare. The nightmare was different this time. He dreamt of walking alongside palm trees. In the near distance, the waves calmly touched the shore. The sand was golden and felt warm against his feet as he walked barefoot. In the dream, he wore a Hawaiian print shirt and knee-length shorts. The perfect attire for a beach vacation. This felt more like a dream than a nightmare; however, soon enough, Joshua's heart began to sink. He just had an ominous feeling that he was being watched.

Peering at the palm trees, he could see a shadowed figure staring at him coldly. He could feel the coldness and felt a drowning feeling in his heart. As the figure saw that he had been caught, he tried to shift slowly back into the shadows. It was too late, however. Joshua had already noticed him but felt it was futile to go after him now.

He already knew who was after him; it wasn't exactly a secret. With this thought in his mind, Joshua began to shift in his sleep. Every dream that he dreamt was subconsciously related to the fears that he had in his real life.

He turned in his sleep as his thoughts became more complex, and at the very last minute, he decided to follow the figure staring at him.

Joshua began running after him and arrived at a clearing. The palm trees had cleared up now, and only sand enveloped the beach.

However, to his disappointment, there was no one in sight. The beach was deserted. Joshua shifted again in his sleep; he was now dangerously teetering at the edge of the rock. Any other sudden move, and he would be plummeting to his death.

In his dream, he began running around, hoping to catch the hooded figure. It was apparent, however, that he had long disappeared in the clearing.

Joshua woke up with a jolt, narrowly escaping death. Down below was a bottomless pit he didn't want to fall in. He woke up carefully, trying not to make any sudden moments. Slowly he climbed down from the boulder, pulling his sleeping bag behind him. Finally sighing with relief, he had just avoided turning into fruit pulp.

He now shifted his focus towards more pertinent matters at hand, i.e. the destination of the lost train and the dream. It's been a while since he had been getting these weird dreams time and time again. Previously, he had comforted himself with the thought that it was just his subconscious projecting itself onto his dreams. He wouldn't be seeing these weird games otherwise. However, Joshua was beginning to get concerned now. Maybe these dreams had more substance than he had previously thought.

His forehead furrowed, and he scratched his head. He felt like he was trapped; turn after turn, he kept getting more lost inside the puzzle instead of finding a way out. A loud stomach rumble interrupted his chain of thoughts, and Joshua placed his hand on his stomach. It was time to get breakfast.

He looked around for some kind of fruit tree or shrub he could eat for breakfast. There was no way he could make the hike down on an empty stomach. He surveyed the area and spotted some berries in a bush. *This will have to do, for now*, he thought to himself. As he was about to grab the berries, he spotted some rabbit hole, which meant that there were some nearby. *Rabbits! They sounded delicious at this time. He had to get them.* Excitedly he grabbed his makeshift spear and went on the hunt for some tantalizing meat.

In a clearing, he found some, nibbling away at some greens. Joshua smiled at himself; he couldn't wait to cook them. *Rabbit and berries go well together; this was going to be an extraordinary meal.*

He waited for the perfect moment before hurling his spear into the innocent rabbit's body. The rabbit didn't know what hit it as it lay bleeding profusely on the forest floor.

Satisfied with his catch, Joshua quickly washed the rabbit with water from his bottle. He had filled up his water bottle with water from the stream for future purposes. Next, he set up a fire using branches and rocks. As the rabbit roasted on the temporary fire he had set up, Joshua cleaned and deseeded the berries. He picked a big leaf to serve as a place and elegantly placed the cut-up berries.

Once the rabbit was done, he cut up its pieces with the help of a sharp rock. It smelled delicious, and Joshua was tempted to dive right in, but he wasn't an animal. Instead, in the style of a true cooking competition contestant, he laid it out artistically on the leaf.

Admiring his handiwork for a minute, Joshua dug into breakfast hungrily. He devoured every morsel until his stomach was satisfied. After breakfast was finished, he was too bloated even to move a muscle. Instead, he decided to stay down for a bit, lying on his back and looking at the glorious sky above. He didn't believe he was actually feeling this way, but he was quite liking this nomadic lifestyle. No one to answer to, no expectations to fulfil. This was the dream.

TREASURE TRAIN

Humming to himself happily, he deiced to make his down and go on another hike. This time he was going towards a more gorgeous destination, which he had spotted from atop the boulder.

Joshua carefully made the journey to the bottom of the hill, all the while admiring the flora and fauna that inhabited the forest floor. He had never been so curious or even had the time to observe anything; that's because he had always been on the run. Now realise that there was life outside of crime and looking sideways at his shoulder, hoping no one was after.

He hummed more loudly now, and it was good to be out in the open where he would finally hear himself hum and think. Where he didn't have to hide his existence for once, he didn't have to shrink himself to survive. Joshua was loving this. He hummed all the way down to the hill. He stopped for a bit to take out his compass from his backpack. It was a Janson compass, rare and very expensive. There was quite a bit of story behind this particular souvenir that he had collected over the years. He had managed to acquire it from a pawn shop. It had caught his eye as he was passing by, and he knew he would get some use out of it.

However, the owner of the shop knew its value and played hardball, almost looting Joshua for it. But he was relentless and didn't budge, and he had decided that he would get the compass, and he was successful.

Smiling to himself, he trudged along the hill, coming to another path that led to the slope that Joshua wanted to climb. Occasionally, he would take sips from his thermos, as it was a hot day. Joshua had quite a good observation, and he looked around for an adequate spot to start digging. He knew he had quite delayed the search for the lost train, and it was high time that he got back on track. He could feel the adrenaline rushing into his system, and he couldn't deny that it felt good to have this feeling back. Joshua hiked for an hour and noticed that the land was even, but it also had a huge amount of hills. He decided to make his way back to the camp. However, on his way back to the campsite and found the perfect spot to start digging. This particular site had fewer trees and could be the potential spot where he would find the train.

Joshua was feeling more and more excited as he approached the clearing. He grabbed his shovel and rushed to search for the lost train.

CHAPTER NINE

DIG

Joshua quickly but cautiously dug through the ground, making sure to be careful of any foreign material that he may find. At this point, he was desperate to search for the lost train, as if his life were dependent on it. The curiosity was now killing him, he had made it his life purpose to find the train, and he was going to do it. It had been dragged long enough.

Frustrated, he let out a long scream and shoved the shovel with all his might into the ground. As the shovel had hit something hard, his shovel deflected back from his hand, twenty feet away from his hand.

Adrenaline rushing through his system, he crept down to see what he had hit. *I finally found it!!* He thought to himself and began to dig with his hands. However, to his sheer disappointment, he saw that it wasn't the top of a train at all. Rather it was just an old metal box that someone had apparently forgotten in the forest. Over the years mother, nature had done her job and made sure to make the box at one with plants and animals. Disgruntled, Joshua sighed and sat on an old tree stub. He was exhausted; the dig had taken a toll on him. Joshua had become so engrossed in the digging that he had even forgotten to look at the time. It was almost evening now, and the sun was setting. He was starting to get hungry again; his stomach craved that rabbit that he had for dinner, and he wished there were more rabbits around.

He got up and looked around hungrily, searching for some kind of animal that could satisfy his hunger. Fortunately, he didn't have to search a lot, as he was lucky enough to find some rabbit holes not far from the site from where he was digging.

He smiled to himself; *today must be my lucky day*. He hungrily leapt towards the hole with his spear, ready to attack. Lo and behold, he found a bunch of rabbits looking at him, petrified. He almost felt ashamed to do it, but his stomach bellowed a loud growl. Swiftly he attacked the biggest looking rabbit while the others scattered in fear. Joshua was satisfied with his kill and quickly started a fire to quench his hunger. This time he didn't have any sides to compliment the rabbit's meat. It had already gotten too dark to look for some berries or other assortments. He would just have to settle for the rabbit's meat for now.

TREASURE TRAIN

Cooked at the perfect temperature, Joshua devoured the rabbit. It was soft, juicy and moist, just how he liked it. The meal was ample, and Joshua felt like it would keep him filled for the coming morning as well. A lot of time had been wasted, and he didn't have a lot of days; this needed to get a move on. He needed to find the train ASAP; everything was on the line if he didn't achieve that.

No, I cannot waste more time; this has gone long enough. He scratched his forehead as beads of sweat covered his face. It was a hot night, and he desperately wanted to bathe in the stream. Unfortunately, there was no stream around here.

If I want to get up early, I should get a move on setting up my tent, and it's already late. He felt tired and dozed off almost immediately in his sleeping tent. It was a chaotic sleep, and Joshua wasn't able to sleep peacefully. Weird dreams enveloped his sleep as much as he tossed and turned. The subconscious mind was projecting disturbing thoughts into his dreams again.

This time he dreamt of digging into a tunnel. It was pitch dark, and Joshua was hurriedly digging away. It was as if he was trapped into some kind of trance, and he couldn't stop digging even if he wanted to. His arms ached with the continuous manual labour, but he kept going on. It felt as if he was controlled by a higher power that he couldn't see nor hear.

Suddenly an earth-shattering noise bellowed from inside the tunnel. A horrendous creature almost the size of a rhino was making a beeline for Joshua. In mere seconds, it collapsed the entire tunnel, creating an easier path for Joshua to reach his goal. However, he now had a bigger obstacle in his way – the creature. Joshua didn't know what to call it; it was massive with grey skin like an alligator with two large tusks protruding from its mouth just like an elephant. It was a mixture of two to three animals, each aspect meshed together, making it uglier than the other.

The animal let out a thunderous growl and charged at Joshua, with a hunger for blood in its red eyes. Joshua knew that he was now done for. Just as the creature hurled towards him, Joshua woke up from his sleep with a jolt. He was dripping from sweat and looked all around the forest. It was completely deserted, but rather than giving it peace, it gave him an uneasy feeling.

After a while, he was able to sleep again. This time he slept peacefully, finally. Joshua woke up the following day refreshed.

It was a new day, and he felt like he could conquer the world. He scoured the area and found a suitable place to start digging to him. It was on top of a hill, and the soil was soft, which required less effort from Joshua. It was an excellent start to a day, and he was feeling hopeful. He just had a good feeling that he would find the missing train today.

Joshua climbed on top of the hill and started his dig; his goal was to create a tunnel that would eventually lead him to the train. It started off as a small hole. However, he was soon knee-deep in soil. He toiled and dug for a few hours until the tunnel completely formed; there was still no sign of the train.

I need to take a break; he thought to himself as he wiped the sweat away from his forehead.

On routine, his stomach began to grumble, and he started to feel hungry. It was time for lunch. Joshua looked around; he didn't have the energy to hunt for a rabbit again, and neither did he feel like having one for the third time.

The only other option was to have berries. He sighed loudly, as he was getting bored of this and missed the urban city lifestyle.

With a heavy look of disappointment, he furrowed for the berries in his backpack and began munching on them. Day by day, he was becoming weaker; if this continued soon, he wouldn't have the strength to accomplish his purpose.

The thought of not completing his purpose haunted him and motivated him to do better. Quickly nibbling on the berries, Joshua gained enough strength to resume his search again. He grabbed his shovel and made a beeline for the partially finished tunnel, continuing his dig.

Joshua wasn't even sure if this was the correct spot. However, he knew that he couldn't stop. No one was forcing him to do this, but he had a strong desire to do this for himself. He didn't know why, but he had a gut feeling that the train was near.

As he dug, the tunnel opened up deeper and broader, and soon enough, Joshua was uprooting trees as big as a house. He knew he was close.

Adrenaline rushed into his system, and he began to dig faster and faster. His body was submerged in sweat as he went deeper into the tunnel.

Suddenly a *CLUNK* interrupted the serene silence of the forest.

TREASURE TRAIN

Joshua rejoiced; it seemed like he had finally found the missing train. He did an energetic victory dance in the air before continuing to dig again.

Suddenly a negative thought crept into his mind, *what if it was another dead end? No, it can't be; it had to be the train. What if he imagined all this? He had been getting weaker and weaker, and everyone knows a weak mind tends to hallucinate.* Joshua's chain of thoughts spiralled, and he felt sick.

Out of the corner of his eye, he began to see shadows and shouted at them. "STOP FOLLOWING ME!!" *He was getting tired of these cat and mouse games; he just wanted to be at peace. Was that too much to ask?*

However, the shadows wouldn't stop chasing him; they kept creeping on him, coming closer and closer. Joshua felt as if he was being suffocated and tried to run away. But they were too strong, surrounding him from all sides; he could feel them closing in on him.

I think this is how I am going to die. Joshua thought as he plunged into darkness, blacking out on the forest floor. There was no one around for miles who could have helped him.

He lay there, easy prey for any passing animal or robber. Soon it began to start raining. However, Joshua wasn't aware of what was happening around him.

It wasn't until dawn the next day that Joshua regained his consciousness. He woke up with a sharp jolt and looked all around him as the events of last night began to seep into his memory.

This couldn't be happening! He began questioning his sanity as he remembered all that had occurred last night. Joshua reevaluated his condition and gave his shovel a long hard stare.

He took some sips from his water bottle and returned to work again. He needed to get this done quickly or slowly; he would lose his sanity and health.

CHAPTER TEN

ON THE ROCKS

Joshua dug vigorously for the whole day. After a day of digging, he managed to create a tunnel of about three and a half feet high. He breathed a sigh of relief. Finally, he was getting somewhere.

This is deep enough to crawl inside, he thought to himself. Joshua gulped; the big moment was upon him, where he could go and finally search for the missing train. It was his dream come true. However, he wasn't feeling as excited and happy as he should have; instead, he felt scared. The train had been abandoned for years; he didn't know what would be awaiting him on the other side. The fact that he was all alone was not helping at all.

But you have always been alone, a voice inside his mind spoke to him. *I'm not too fond of it, though.* Soon enough, Joshua was having a conversation with himself. *This was his dream; he couldn't just let it go because of his fear. And it wasn't something to be scared of. The one thing he had learned in his life was that sweet, precious victory was on the other side of fear.* Joshua decided to forget his fears and crawl into the tunnel; he had not lived in the forest for so long to return home empty-handed.

The tunnel was relatively cooler than the forest and darker too. Luckily, he had ordered an industry-grade small flashlight from Amazon just before this journey. He was geared up. He had also gotten extra batteries in case of any emergency.

Funnily, he had gotten so many batteries that his bag felt like he was carrying a hundred kilos worth of products. Some kids had also made fun of him, pointing to his back as the adults looked in awe at the bag he carried all by himself. Surprisingly, Joshua had liked the attention, and he ended, he remembered as he smirked to himself.

He climbed into the tunnel and started crawling, taking the direction the tunnel took him in. The flashlight was very bright and made it easier for him to navigate his way. It was pitch dark, and his heart pounded in his chest wildly. Any moment now, something would leap at him.

Joshua pushed his fears aside and pummelled into the tunnel. The tunnel expanded into a bigger room at the edge, and Joshua braced himself for the landing. If the train were inside this tunnel, it would be here now. His heart was now beating faster than ever as he pushed through the dirt.

Suddenly, the tunnel surface gave way, and Joshua plummeted inside a big ditch.

AAAAAAHHHHHHHH! He screamed at the top of his lungs as he began fearing how deep the fall would be and if he would make it out alive. Joshua fell on his face, covered in dust and dirt. He spat some dirt out of his mouth and struggled to get up. His left shoulder hurt as he tried to move it, he felt a sharp pang. Muttering under his breath in anger, he grabbed the first aid box from his backpack and attempted to bandage his injured arm.

This is a pain! He thought to himself, that moving along with one arm would be much more work than it already was. He wiped the beads of sweat that were forming on his forehead. *Maybe he was too old for this now.*

He furrowed his eyebrows. *This was no time for self-pity; he was this close to turning his dream into a reality.* Wincing in pain, he got up and dusted the dirt off his clothes. As he saw what lay ahead of him, he exclaimed in horror.

Corpses and skeletons littered the place; it seemed that no one had gotten lucky enough to find the treasure.

This was going to be much harder than I thought; he saw the littered bodies. Thousands of people had tried and failed to retrieve it. *How could he believe that he would he can be successful?* His self-doubts were beginning to creep on him again. Flustered, he sat down and drank water from his thermos.

Looking around at the corpses and their belongings, there was a vast difference. Some seemed they had come to find the train decades ago, while there were some who only looked like a year or two older. Scratching his head, he got up and began examining them. *Maybe there was something of importance that he could use later; they appeared to give the impression of knowledgable beings. Although not knowledgable enough to avoid a misfortune.*

Joshua quickly went through all of their things to see if there was something that he could salvage. Unfortunately, there was very little. He did find some money. However, it was decades old. Maybe it could be worth millions of dollars now and end up making me rich. It is worth a shot if the train thing didn't work out. He also found some texts and manuscripts regarding the train that helped him know more about the challenges he was about to face.

TREASURE TRAIN

According to them, the train was a thousand years old. No one had been successful in finding where it was buried. Some had given up all their life in search but didn't come up with anything fruitful. Those who had successfully found the deserted treasure train faced a wretched fate that took their lives. Joshua read this in a petrified tone; he didn't want to suffer the same fate as his predecessors.

For a while, he just sat stunned. He didn't know how to proceed. If he went further on his mission, there was a chance that he would not make it out alive.

I have come this far, haven't I? It is my dream I have to achieve it. With this conviction in mind, he started to look around again. *There must be something here that I can use to help me go further.* He surveyed the room, and what he saw made his heart nearly jump with excitement.

At the west end was a large circular opening filled with rocks about the size of sandbags. *Could this be the entrance to the lost train? Could he be this lucky?* Excited, he ran towards the clearing, moving the rocks one by one in hopes of some kind of clue that would lead him to the train.

Joshua began to clear out the rocks; he figured that he would lift enough to make a small space for him to squeeze in. The rocks weren't heavy, and he had made ample space for himself in a short time. Grabbing his flashlight, he peered inside the makeshift tunnel. He didn't want anything attacking him by surprise.

It seemed like he had stepped into an abandoned german bunker from World War II, used by Nazi soldiers. According to his compass, the tunnel led him further away from Walbrzych. He gripped a twine from his backpack, tied it around a rock and began his climb down to the tunnel. The tunnel was flooded in pitch darkness, and as he started his tract, he estimated a climb of about twenty to forty feet.

It was a dangerous expedition and one that he needed a lot of willpower and strength to make it out alive. Climbing down, he almost tripped on a large piece of metal that was sticking out of the ground.

Cursing under his breath, he looked at it closely, and his heart almost did a double take. They were train tracks! He couldn't believe that he had been so lucky. Baffled, he ran his hand through his hair; never had he won anything in his life. Now he was on his way to becoming the wealthiest man on earth. *Could*

TREASURE TRAIN

this really be happening?

If this worked out, he would change his mentality and start to consider himself the luckiest man. He had always cursed Lady Luck for his bad fate. However, doubts began to form in his head once again.

It's better not to tempt fate and think ahead. Maybe these are train tracks that wouldn't lead anywhere. He came to his senses and counted his eggs before they hatched.

Without further ado, he followed the tunnel. It had begun to expand, and there was now enough space for him to stand. It increased to the size of a small house in front of Joshua's eyes.

However, as Joshua continued walking on the path, the tunnel began to narrow. After walking for quite a while, he came across another circle of rocks, each the size of small sandbags. It was similar to the one before. This time, however, he didn't have the energy to move the rocks and wished that a strong gust of wind would follow through and carry them for him.

Joshua took a small break and ate a snack bar, some blueberries and a few gulps of water. His water supply was running short, and he didn't know how long would he have to live under the tunnel trying to reach the lost train. After the ordeal and hard work, he felt tired and decided to take a nap before continuing forward.

CHAPTER ELEVEN
IT WAS LIKE A ROOM

Joshua woke up abruptly from his deep slumber. Awaking with a jolt, he looked around his surroundings. It took him a moment to realize where he was and what he was doing.

The makeshift room was pitch dark, and he had a strong inclination that there were bats on the ceiling. There was little to no ventilation, and if he hadn't had his watch on him, he wouldn't be able to tell day and night apart.

Joshua sighed loudly; he was this close to making his lifelong dream come true. However, as he progressed, things kept getting harder and harder.

I have always dreamed of finding the whereabouts of the lost train; I can't give up now. His thoughts were interrupted by a loud rumble from his stomach. He glanced meekly at his bag because he knew he was running short of it, and there were only two choices ahead of him. Either he could continue his journey without food or water because, from the looks of it, the tunnel wasn't ending anytime soon. Or he could go back and fill his rations of food and water. There was one problem with the latter; he didn't have the energy to go back and forth. Even though this was his dream, he didn't quite look forward to the hard work and toil that he had to go through to achieve it.

His thoughts racing, he reached for his bag and glanced at the contents inside. The bag contained half a sandwich, two protein bars, a handful of berries and half a bottle of water. These would last him, at most for two days, that too if he only ate once a day. His stomach grumbled as he thought about it; he wasn't used to going hungry and was used to having a big meal. This was going to be a challenge.

Looking at his watch, he saw that it was almost midday. *I need to get going; I can't loiter around like this all day.* He took out a protein bar from his bag and munched on it while figuring out his next step.

The narrow tunnel was opening into another passageway, it was small, but luckily Joshua had lost weight due to his special diet these days. He slipped in easily through the narrow hole, blinking as his eyes adjusted to the new space. He was surprised to see what lay before his eyes. This room was completely different from the previous one. It was roughly the size of a school bus. Contrary to the previous one, this room was well-lit and had good exposure to sunlight and ventilation.

Entering the room made Joshua feel lighter as his breathing normalized. The tunnel was suffocating, but thankfully this room wasn't like the others. He busied himself and examined the room.

Unusually, it was full of trunks and paintings. The trunks he understood, but it was odd to see paintings buried underneath a tunnel. The more he explored the place, the more he realized that it seemed more and more like a warehouse used to store valuables.

And to think, most of the world isn't even aware of the treasure that lies beneath them! He chuckled to himself. Even if he didn't discover the train and its treasures, these paintings alone would sell for millions. Delivering and transporting them, however, will be a headache. He scrutinized the paintings; they mainly comprised of all sizes and subjects. All of them were carefully packed away as if someone had predicted the train's demise and wanted to keep the paintings safe no matter what happened. They were packed with such care and love that it took a while to unpack one or two. He chose to unpack two of the smallest ones that he could find.

Joshua was amazed at the craftsmanship and the expertise of the artists. The brush strokes were delicate and abrupt, as if each was telling its own story. It was a still life of a vase, flowers and fruits.

This is the most stunning still life he had set his eyes on. *If I ever get out of this alive, I would get this painting for my house, for sure.* He vowed to himself. He often thought of his perfect home, as he was tired of this nomadic lifestyle. Tired of running, he wanted to settle down, preferably with a family. That was the dream!

Right, I have to work for it. No one wants to live with a fugitive on the run, with the police breathing down his neck. He still hadn't figured out the part where the police would cease to look for him. But he was sure he would think of something to keep them quiet. The one thing that he knew was that he could no longer live in fear, that someone or something was constantly watching him. *He was exhausted from living this life. Hopefully, everything would go well, and he could retire as a thief. Soon he would be living the dream!*

He continued to unwrap the paintings from the blankets. The

white blankets had developed a yellowish tinge from being kept under the ground for so long. Joshua got so busy admiring the paintings that he forgot about the trunks for just a moment.

Opening the trunks, he realized they were not ordinary. But they were his ticket to the life he had always wanted. Each of the trunks was filled with jewels, diamonds, coins and wads of Reichsmarks. His eyes shone as he looked at the treasure that lay in front of him. He felt that his luck had finally opened up.

Standing in the middle of the room, Joshua was surrounded by paintings, jewels and huge lumps of cash. If he successfully managed to take this out of the tunnel and exchange it for the current currency, he would be a wealthy millionaire. *Heck no, a billionaire! There was enough money in this tunnel to feed a small country every day for years.*

Joshua rummaged through the treasure and came across another priceless treasure. It was an antique painting by the famous artist Vincent Van Gogh; his signature brushstrokes were all over the painting. He was one of Joshua's favourite artists. To find this painting among the lost treasure was a miracle, to say the least. He didn't expect that he would find it here of all places.

He instantly grabbed it, pleased to see that it was in great shape. It was also small enough to squeeze through the tunnel's narrow passages. Joshua decided it was time to capitalize on the situation and head to the surface.

According to his watch, it was late afternoon now, and he needed to get a move on. This had been delayed enough, and these should be sold to help Joshua financially.

After a somewhat treacherous journey that led him back to the forest floor, Joshua was able to breathe a sigh of relief. He secured the painting in its makeshift scrap of a blanket and buried it under a tree for safety.

Like an alarm, his stomach gave a loud rumble, alerting him that it was time for lunch/dinner, depending on whatever timetable he was following.

Joshua walked over to the campsite, filling his water bottle repeatedly until satisfied. After fulfilling his thirst, he bathed in the stream. He felt a different kind of glee as he swam and became one with nature.

Not having the energy to hunt, he ate a light meal of berries and protein bars. *I can hunt something in the morning; for now, I need to sleep and gain strength for the next chapter in my life.*

Deeply absorbed in his thoughts, he drifted off to sleep. His dreams were filled with pursuits to cash the famous painting and ultimately make him rich beyond his wildest dreams.

CHAPTER TWELVE
GOING TO TOWN

As morning dawned, Joshua sleepily opened his eyes. It was a new day, and he was excited to finish his plan. The possession of the invaluable Vincent Van Gogh kickstarted his dreams of being rich.

Rubbing his eyes lazily, he went to the tree where he had buried the painting. He quickly dug it out from its hiding place, relieved to find it snuggled in its blanket. In the back of his mind, he feared someone must have stolen it while he was still asleep. Thankfully, he was all alone here.

But for how long? He was sure that the police were still on the search for him. Not to mention, he wasn't known to be on his best behaviour with the locals. He had undoubtedly shaken the feathers in the wrong way of more than a few people.

Worried, Joshua's forehead furrowed; he needed to cash the painting and escape. This is where things got complicated; he didn't know how he would become a seller – without disclosing his identity.

TREASURE TRAIN

Beads of sweat formed on his forehead as he started to think about the exodus. He had been waiting all his life for the sweet release from all his burdens. Joshua sighed deeply; he was closer to his destiny than he could have thought. However, the path was getting harder and harder. And he wasn't sure if he would make it.

Well, I will have to try; I didn't come all this way to give up in the end. There were two ways he could go about selling the painting. First, he would have to post the listing through an art gallery as an anonymous seller. Two, he could convince someone who doesn't have trouble hiding their identity to post on his behalf.

However, he will have to share his profits in the second option, and he wasn't very keen on doing that. The former sounded better; he could keep all the profits without revealing his identity.

The only aspect that scared him was that there was more risk involved. But, hey, no risk, no gain. I didn't come this far to play it safe. *Let's get to work!*

The first step in his elaborate plan consisted of building a sturdy campsite that would serve as a dependable shelter. It should be easier to spot, even from afar, as his schedule will be unpredictable.

Joshua set to work; he made a makeshift pole from a thin branch, and attaching the raggedy white blanket, he fashioned a pole. He pushed it deep into the mud right in front of his tent, ensuring it was easily visible from all distances. Next, he needed a map. Now he had never been to the forest before; this was his first time in this city. However, he had explored the woods, and thanks to his strong memory, he may be able to draft a map. He started from the meeting point where the city merges into the forest. That gave him a clear vantage point. Joshua next mapped out the precise directions to the campsite from all corners of the woods. The map indicated the way to the tunnel, which he needed to ensure was accurate. He couldn't afford to get lost and miss out on the treasure he had searched far and wide. To make it easy for himself, he labelled the stream and the spots where he discovered the most succulent meat. *These are important for survival in the forest*, he thought to himself.

Carefully placing the map in his backpack, he started preparing for his journey ahead. The next course of action was to take a taxi to the city where he could sell his priceless painting.

TREASURE TRAIN

Although he had to be extra cautious, Joshua knew it wasn't impossible. The tricky part was yet to begin.

Selling it anonymously would be a challenging feat to achieve. He needed to make sure not to attract the attention of the locals. It was hard enough that the drastic contrast was clearly written on his face, marking him as one of the foreigners. To conceal his appearance, he took out a cap and a pair of sunglasses from his bag. It was casual and not extreme as well, the perfect guise for a secret mission. Feeling better about his appearance, Joshua made his way out of the forest and towards the city's outskirts. He waited by the side of the road to hail a taxi, the painting carefully wrapped in the blanket – tightly tucked in his arm.

It was a typical day in the town of Czechia, and Joshua was quickly able to blend in the hustle and bustle. Hailing the taxi would be more complicated than he had thought, as there was a lot of commotion. The last thing that he wanted was to attract attention. If anyone even saw the painting, it would be a disaster for him.

He was sure that it wasn't only him who recognized the worth of the painting. Several others would be able to distinguish its value and try to get their hands on it. As an ulterior course of action, he waited patiently for a taxi, careful not to seem urgent.

At long last, one taxi driver stopped in front of him, lowering his window to inquire about his location.

"Where to?"

Joshua thought for a moment, he knew where he wanted to go, but he wasn't sure if it would be the best course of action to go there directly.

"There is this famous bar near Pod Homolkou 85; ah, I forgot the name." He pretended to be in deep thought as he tried to recall the name.

The driver rushed to his aid, ensuring he would book his ride. The roads were nearly empty now as it was almost noon.

"Are you referring to the infamous Picadilly Bar?" He asked inquisitively.

"Yes! That's the one." Joshua answered excitedly as if going to this bar would be his life's mission – an achievement without which his bucket list wouldn't be complete.

TREASURE TRAIN

As if he was reading his mind, the driver replied. "The Picadilly bar is so famous; many people want to visit it once in their lifetime. In fact, it is on their bucket list." He finished matter-of-factly.

Joshua wasn't in the mood for small talk, so he nodded along. Other important things were on his mind that needed to be sorted out immediately. He didn't have time to dilly-dally. Placing the painting on his lap, he sat in the taxi. He could tell the driver was inclined to talk more about the city's rich culture, but he simply cut him off.

"Just drop me off at the nearest block; I can walk from there."

Soon enough, he had arrived at his destination, The Picadilly Bar. It was one of the grandest locations of Czeich, popular among the locals and tourists alike. Slowly, he walked towards the bar after paying the driver.

Right around the corner was the local art gallery. Although it was humble, the one good aspect was that it had links to Sotheby's – the world's most prominent and influential gallery. The only problem was that it was located in London, unreachable for Joshua.

He entered through the rustic gates, taking in the aroma of old canvas and oil paints. Almost instantly, an attendant was there to assist him, looking at him questioningly. He assumed it was because of his ill-clad demeanour; clients who had million-dollar paintings to sell would usually come in suits and jewels. Ignoring his look, he unfolded the painting from its blanket.

"I have got a little something of value that might interest," Joshua trailed off, trying to capture his attention.

The attendant merely sighed tiredly. He had seen about a dozen of these this week alone. All of them turned out to be counterfeit. Taking out his magnifying glass, he started to examine the painting. His careless glances suddenly became scrutinized looks.

"This is the real deal! How did you get your hands on it? It has been pronounced to be lost for over decades."

"I just got lucky, I guess." Joshua grinned for the first time in days. "How much do you think it would sell for?"

"It should go for a whopping ten million dollars, according to my estimation."

Joshua felt like hugging him; this was the best news he had

heard. "Put it up immediately on sale; both of us will become rich."

After a week ago, Joshua received a call from the gallery. The painting had sold for an astounding amount of eighteen and a half million dollars. Joshua was shocked when he heard this; finally, he would live the life he had always dreamt of. A grand and luxurious lifestyle, fit for a king.

www.ingramcontent.com/pod-product-compliance
Lightning Source LLC
Chambersburg PA
CBHW030544130626
46552CB00006B/2409